THE 13TH PROSPECT STRANDED ON STONY ISLAND

A BLACK LOVE DETECTIVE STORY
BOOK 6

ANTWAN FLOYD SR.

CRIME FICTION MEDIA

ALSO BY ANTWAN FLOYD SR.

BLACK LOVE DETECTIVE NOVELS

Piece Keeper

Cannibal in the City

Body Bags & Last Rites

A Pound of Flesh, An Ounce of Blood

The Detective and the Criminal

The 13th Prospect Stranded on Stony Island

Crew Love

Crew Love pt. 2 "The Black Mob"

Dope Fiction "Alpha Female"

Dope Fiction pt. 2 "Sigma Female"

Dope Fiction pt. 3 Beta Female

Wild 100's

Sperm Donor

The Last Transmission of a Gangster

Danielle Lovelace Vigilante for Hire

Purple Reign "A Trigger Brown Mystery"

Dead Before Morning "Rhys & Tilly Series Book 1"

The Addiction "An Anthology"
12 Months of Murder: Introduction to Seduction
12 Months of Murder: Reasonable Doubt
12 Months of Murder: The Life and Times of Jade Leskiv Vol. 1

ONE

"How did we get here?" the towering figure asked, his voice low and almost detached as he stood face to face with the frightened woman. Her wide eyes were frozen in terror, darting from his cold, expressionless face to his hands, which slowly wrapped around her neck.

He squeezed.

Her fingers, desperate and clawing at his arms, found no purchase. His grip only tightened as he pressed her body forcefully against the wall. She gasped, choking, eyes pleading for mercy. He stared into her, repeating his question as if genuinely searching for an answer.

"How did we get here?"

A smirk creased his lips as he felt her fight begin to fade. The frantic scratching of her nails grew weaker, her arms falling limp by her sides. A sick thrill shot through him, not just from the power he held over her but from the deeper realization that this—this was what made him feel alive. The control. The dominance. In these moments, when life dangled by his hands, the emptiness he often felt receded. This was all he knew anymore—pain, suffering, control—and he clung to it like a lifeline.

A deep-rooted shame stirred somewhere inside, but he quickly smothered it. He had told himself for years that there was no going back, no redemption. What was left of him was just this—the violence, the darkness. As much as it revolted him, it also defined him.

"Why are you doing this to me?" he asked mockingly, his voice soft, almost whispering. It was a question not for her but for himself. He had asked it a hundred times, a thousand, but he never found an answer. Not one that satisfied him. He wasn't here for revenge or even for the money—though that's what he told himself, what he told his crew. The truth was uglier, buried deep under layers of denial.

He squeezed harder, his breath becoming ragged. Her legs buckled beneath her, and she slouched against the wall, all fight gone. He felt a rush of something primal as he let her fall to the floor, collapsing alongside her, still holding on, still squeezing as if releasing her would mean releasing himself from the only thing he could control.

His eyes bulged, saliva dripped from his lips, pooling on his chin as he felt her life slip away. His body responded, disgustingly, as he climaxed in his pants. The act, vile and uncontrollable, was both a release and a punishment.

Panting and out of breath, he slowly released his grip and stood, looking down at her lifeless body. A deep, hollow emptiness returned almost instantly, creeping into his chest like an unwelcome guest.

"I expected more of a fight," he muttered to himself, feeling no satisfaction, only a growing void.

The silence that followed was punctuated by a voice from behind him, dragging him back to reality.

"What now, boss?"

He didn't answer at first, staring blankly down at her, his thoughts a swirling mess of guilt, power, and self-loathing. Finally, after a long pause, he wiped the saliva from his chin and spoke, his voice flat and emotionless.

"Search the place. See if you can find anything that'll point me to my money."

As the other man moved into action, the towering figure stood there, staring at the body, feeling nothing but a faint echo of the question that always gnawed at him.

Why?

Two

Amanda Moore's frantic race against the clock was a symphony of anxiety. Each breath felt shallow, her pulse a constant, erratic drumbeat in her ears. She chain-smoked three Newports in rapid succession, the harsh nicotine bite doing little to calm her nerves. Her hand shook as she took a quick sip of wine, hoping it would steady her, ground her in the chaos. The glass clinked unsteadily as she set it down on the counter, her lips dry despite the alcohol.

In the mirror, she paused, assessing herself with surgical precision. Every detail had to be perfect—no room for mistakes today. The makeup was just right, thick enough to mask the sleepless nights etched under her eyes but not so heavy it would raise suspicion. She tilted her head, checking from every angle, ensuring nothing peeked through. She couldn't afford to slip up, not now.

Her eyes darted back to the clock on the wall. Time was running out. She gave her apartment a quick once-over, scanning for anything that might seem out of place. Her mind raced with a thousand details—*Did I lock the back door? Is the window still open? Did I leave any evidence?* She didn't trust herself to remember.

Amanda's keys lay by the entrance, a silent beacon of escape. She reached for them, hesitated, and then flung open the closet. She needed something to hide the scars on her neck from the scuffle. Her mind wandered to Sheek and the mess she'd gotten herself into. She thought she had outplayed him, thought she could keep her daughter safe, but everything was unraveling faster than she could contain it.

What am I doing?

Amanda's hand hesitated on the closet door handle, her mind racing too fast to remember what lay behind it. She flung it open, searching for her silk scarf to hide the bruising on her neck—and then the body lurched forward, falling toward her like a nightmare come to life.

She stifled a scream, her heart seizing as the dead weight nearly knocked her off balance. The corpse—his corpse—slumped awkwardly, the lifeless eyes half-open, staring blankly at her. The knife was still buried in his chest, a grim reminder of the fight she'd barely survived.

This wasn't supposed to happen. Her gaze lingered on the corpse—her mind raced. She'd been so careful, planned every detail, moved to a new place, and kept her head down. But here she was, and now there was no turning back. A breathless prayer escaped her lips as she sealed the closet door, shutting away the grisly secret inside.

In over her head, she realized now how naive she'd been to think she could outwit Sheek. Amanda had believed she'd evaded detection, that she could lay low until she figured out her next move. But reality hit hard. Her options were dwindling fast. Her daughter's phone had been silent all morning, and fear gnawed at her from the inside. They'd talked last night, her daughter had promised to flee to Milwaukee to stay with a friend. Amanda had clung to that hope, convincing herself her daughter had escaped the city, that she'd be safe.

But hope was all she had. Until her daughter called. Exiting her place and locking the apartment door, she headed towards the exit "Hold the door!" A man called out as she rushed toward her car. He had a slight African accent—she didn't know which country he was from, and it didn't matter. His voice grated against her frazzled nerves. She didn't turn around, didn't even glance at him. She let the security door slam shut behind her with a satisfying thud, locking him out as she hustled toward her car.

The man stood behind the door, holding a box in his arms, shaking his head in annoyance.

"Damn foreigners," Amanda muttered under her breath, her mind racing back to the situation inside.

Her heart still pounded as she unlocked the car and slipped inside, hands gripping the wheel. There was no room for mistakes now. She was running out of time. And out of options.

THREE

T he Greyhound bus rumbled into the garage at 630 W. Harrison St., and Yehohanan Daniels waited patiently, his weathered face betraying no emotion as the other passengers gathered their belongings and disembarked. Seated at the back of the bus, he paid little mind to the stares he received from the other passengers. After enduring a grueling thirty-hour journey from Ocala, Florida, with multiple transfers, he was relieved to have finally reached his destination: Chicago. A city he hadn't set foot in for fifty-five years.

Back then, the world was a different place. The Chicago he remembered was a volatile, racially divided city, caught in the throes of the Civil Rights Movement. He had left as a boy, but now he returned as an old man, aged beyond his years. The city had changed. Hell, the entire world had changed. And yet, despite the years and distance, the ghosts of his past felt just as close.

Yehohanan's imposing presence still commanded attention: a bald head, a long, grizzled beard, and a face adorned with tattoos, each one telling its own story of survival, regret, and violence. If that wasn't enough to intimidate most, the prison uniform, a stark reminder of his fifty-five years behind bars for murder, certainly did the job. Some of the passengers gave him wide-eyed glances, while others quickly averted their eyes, pretending they hadn't noticed the grim figure at the back of the bus.

His prison clothes had been replaced, but not by choice. The state didn't care much for formalities when releasing someone who'd spent more than half a century locked away. He had heard stories of men who had served long sentences being sent home still wearing their prison garb, without a single loved one waiting for them. If you lacked family to greet you at the gates with fresh clothes, you left with nothing more than the state's parting gift: a bus ticket, a meager check, and your release papers—papers that might be your only salvation if the law stopped you on the outside.

Yehohanan patted his pockets, making sure he still had the $1,500 check the prison had cut him and the crumpled release papers that had become as essential as a second skin. Losing those papers would be like losing his last shred of identity. With a final look around the now-empty bus, he extended his hand to the driver in a firm, deliberate handshake.

"Thanks for getting us here safely, sir," he said, his voice deep and gravelly, the sound of someone who hadn't had much reason to speak in the last fifty years.

The young Black driver met his gaze, the age difference between them stark. "You're welcome, and welcome home, man. Good luck out there."

Home. The word didn't sit right with him. He nodded and stepped off the bus, his boots touching Chicago soil for the first time since he was a teenage boy. The city had grown in ways he couldn't fully grasp. Skyscrapers towered over the streets, and there were more people, more noise—everything faster, more congested. The cars, the fashion, the very air seemed alien. Even the terminal, bustling with travelers, felt like a different world. People of all races and backgrounds moved freely, their eyes fixed on glowing screens. He couldn't help but think about how foreign all this would have seemed to the boy he once was, a kid caught in the fury of segregation, hatred, and fear.

Fifty-five years ago, he'd been just fifteen when they threw him in with grown men. The Civil Rights Movement was at its height, but he was no activist. He was a scared white boy from the Southside, trying to do what he thought was right. He could still remember the fear in her eyes—Amanda, a pregnant Black girl not much older than him, cornered by three men in an alleyway. They wanted to hurt her for no reason other than the color of her skin. She was pregnant, carrying life, and yet they only saw her as an object to torment. He'd grabbed the nearest thing he could find—an old steel pipe—and when they came at him, he didn't stop swinging until one of them lay dead at his feet.

They didn't see him as a hero. They didn't care that he had saved Amanda's life. To them, he was a murderer. A white boy who'd crossed a line that wasn't meant to be crossed. The trial was quick, brutal. The judge spared him from the death sentence, but only just. He spent his entire adult life in prison, a relic of a time most had long since forgotten. He never thought he'd make it out. Never believed this day would come.

Yehohanan's eyes scanned the crowd for his ride, but there was no familiar face. He stood there, feeling like a ghost in a world that had left him behind. The terminal was a whirlwind of activity, filled with people of all ages, some curled up on the floor with their luggage, others walking dogs on leashes—leashes in a bus station, of all things. In his mind, it was still 1960. The world had been simpler, though not necessarily kinder. The buildings were shorter, the streets less crowded. And back then, if a white boy protected a Black girl, he was throwing his life away.

He glanced around, his eyes searching for a payphone, but they were nowhere to be found. He hadn't expected that. Payphones were everywhere back then. Now, all he saw were people with glowing screens pressed against their ears or tapping away on little handheld devices. He was a relic in a world full of things he didn't understand.

With no other option, Yehohanan made his way to a quiet spot on the staircase, settling down as if he had no place better to be. He had waited fifty-five years. What was a few more minutes?

He sat, feeling the weight of the world around him, but also the weight of the past, of the life he had lost. He had saved Darlene, but in doing so, he had lost everything. The city, this life—it wasn't his anymore. He wasn't sure it ever had been.

FOUR

wo weeks had passed and still no word from Pepper Red, just like when he was a kid, she disappeared without a trace. He would never admit it, but it bothered him more than he liked. Parking in front of his detective agency he marveled at the property, an old church that he rehabbed. He had only been in business a year or so and it was going well so far. He went inside, he was surprised to see the kids there.

"What are you two doing here on a Sunday?" Black asked Johnny and Joanne.

"Just chilling," Johnny said, not looking up from his phone. Johnny was his impromptu foster child for the time being. The nephew of an Irish gangster. Black still couldn't believe he had custody of a teenager, a white teenager at that. Joanne had yet to respond.

"And what about you?" Black asked directed towards Joanne. "You know I'm not paying you for today."

Joanne was his secretary, he hired her as a favor to a client. She laughed. She was sitting on the sofa with a stack of books beside her. "I know, I like to come here and study, it's a chill vibe."

Black laughed. "Yall some weird kids."

"What?" Joanne asked locking eyes with Black, a smile across her face.

"Why aren't you guys outside doing something?"

"Something like what?" She asked.

"Shit, I don't know, roller skating, shooting pool, go to the gym or a park and play basketball, you know an actual physical activity."

"I'm good," Johnny said, face still glued to his phone.

"At least she's doing homework, where's your books at?"

"I left em at school."

"So, you didn't have any homework on Friday?"

"I did."

"And?"

"I'll do it tomorrow in class."

"That's not how this shit works."

"I don't follow, as long as I turn it in, right?"

"Wrong, if you're doing shit from last week, you're not paying attention to the shit being taught that day."

"I'll be straight."

"Nah, lil homie, you are going to step your shit up when it comes to school."

Johnny didn't respond. Black walked over and knocked his phone out of his hands. Johnny bulked up at Black. "What you tripping for man, I heard you."

"Next time look at me when I'm talking to you, and when I say something to your ass you respond, you hear me?"

Johnny and Black locked eyes, after an intense stare-down Johnny relented and lowered his eyes. "Yes sir."

"And let some of that air out your chest, you buck up at me again, it's not going to end well."

Johnny relaxed his shoulders and lowered his eyes once more. Spoke in a mumbled tone. "Yes sir."

He walked over and picked up his phone, caught eyes with Joanne, who remained silent during the interaction, she smirked at him and shook her head disapprovingly. Johnny smiled and flipped her the bird.

"See that's your problem right there, you think everything is a joke." She said as she went back to reading her textbook.

The bell rang, and Black looked over at the teens. "You two expecting anyone?"

"As a matter of fact, I am," Joanne said as she stood and began making her way towards the door. "A potential client."

Black didn't respond, he leaned against the wall, folded his arms across his chest as Joanne returned with her guest.

"This is my accounting Professor, Professor Moore, Professor Moore this is my boss Mr. Love."

Black stuck out his hand to shake hands with the elder woman, she took his hand into hers and shook. Black offered a curt smile. "What can I do for you?"

"Excuse us," Joanne said as she gathered her books and followed Johnny into the kitchen.

"Joanne speaks very highly of you."

Black waved off her compliment. "You know kids, put way more on it than there needs to be."

"Don't be modest, I've seen the news reports and YouTube videos online, very impressive. I was delighted when I found out that Joanne worked for you and thought that you would be ideal to help me with my predicament."

"Please, have a seat." Black gestured towards the sofa where Joanne was sitting.

Professor Moore shook her head no. "Won't be long. I have a $5,000 dollar deposit and another $5,000 once the job is done."

"Before we get to money, what's the job?"

"I need you to set up a meeting, nothing major."

Black smirked. "$5,000, nothing major?"

"Almost nothing."

"Who is the meeting with?"

"A gentleman by the name of Sheek Green."

"I'm familiar with him."

"Good, all I need is for you to-"

"Hold up, that's going to be a hard no."

"You haven't even let me finish."

"No need, whatever it is, I'm not getting involved."

"Joanne told me you'd help me."

"She shouldn't have, I'll talk to her about that later."

She unzipped her purse and removed five stacks of crisp hundred-dollar bills.

Black held both hands up shaking his head no. "Like I said, not going to happen, sorry you came over for nothing, I'll have Joanne see you out." Professor Moore placed the cash back into her purse and zipped it closed. Black continued. "Joanne!" He yelled out as he took his position back against the wall. Joanne came out. "The professor is leaving." Joanne took her gently by the arm and led her back to the door, walking her outside to her car. Black walked over to the door and watched as the two women talked by her car. Johnny came from the kitchen still looking down at his phone as he spoke.

"You did the right thing."

"What's that?"

"Not taking that case."

"Don't be listening to my conversations."

"Sorry."

Black turned and faced Johnny. "What do you know about him, your uncle do business with him?"

"Nah, but they spoke."

"Was it cordial?"

"For the most part."

"Tell me about it."

"I came in on the butt end of the conversation, had just got in from school stopped by the bar to see Uncle Mickey and he was there."

"What happened?"

"Heard something about the Sheek fella telling Uncle Mickey he was going to start carrying his beers from his microbrewery on tap and get rid of most of the big brand names."

Black chuckled. "Oh yeah, how did Mickey take that?"

"Honestly better than I thought. There was no bloodshed and Sheek walked out of there on his own."

"Yeah, that's surprising on Sheek's end too, not many say no to him. He has a chain of neighborhood bars it's alleged he muscled in on Chatham, Riverdale, Grand Crossing, Austin, Harvey, Englewood, and Lawndale, with his flagship bar in Rock Island. With spots in Des Moines and Water Loo, Iowa. It's not surprising that he was looking to expand to other markets in Chicago, and Mickey said no...from what I hear Sheek doesn't usually fold."

"Yeah, well, neither does my Uncle Mickey."

***

After checking in at the office, Black had more stops to make, with Stone's place being the first on his list. He parked outside her apartment at 4451 S. Princeton and glanced at his phone as a text message popped up.

"What's going on with you, Black?"

The text was from Deborah Kiss, the medical examiner he was seeing. It was still a new relationship, and he decided to ignore the message. Instead, he sent a text to Stone and then got out of the car. Stone soon appeared at her door, and Black headed over to greet her. Another text arrived from Deborah.

"Fuck you too!"

Black ignored that text as well and followed Stone up the stairs. He had made many trips up those stairs over the years, and it typically ended in her bedroom. However, this time was different. Stone stopped at the table in the living room and took a seat. Black joined her, realizing that he had never sat in this room before. Her kids were usually around, and the apartment had always been bustling. Today, it seemed empty.

"So, what's up?" Stone asked, locking eyes with Black.

"Shit, just checking on you and the baby. Y'all good?"

She ran her hands across her stomach, which was showing more prominently now, and smiled. "We're fine."

"Cool. You eat?"

"Nah, just snacking here and there. Got a craving for a pizza puff, fries, and mild sauce."

"That sounds good."

"I know, right?"

"Run and get us some."

She frowned. "Not funny, Black." He let out a light laugh, but she continued. "You need to start doing more, Black."

"More like what, Stone?"

"You come over here empty-handed."

"Am I supposed to have something when I slide through?"

She rolled her eyes. "Never mind."

Black pushed his chair back from the table. "Here you go."

"Yeah, here I go, don't worry about it."

"I'm not, because you ain't told me what's on your mind."

"I shouldn't have to."

"Let's pretend you do."

She stood from the table, placing her hands on her hips. "Babies need stuff, Black. Diapers, diaper bags, bottles, car seats... What are you going to wait until the baby gets here to start getting things?"

"Nah, but—"

"But what, Black? You don't even feed me or your child. I say I want a pizza puff, and you're making jokes and shit. If I was ready to fuck, you'd be singing a different tune, right?"

"I know you ain't tripping over a funky-ass pizza puff."

At this point, their voices were getting louder, and Sapphire, Stone's oldest daughter, stepped out of her bedroom, taking Black by surprise. She looked nothing like her mother. While Stone was short, barely five feet, and petite with short hair, Sapphire was statuesque, athletically toned, with long blonde extension braids. She had just graduated from high school and was starting her freshman year in college. Black barely acknowledged her as he turned his attention back to Stone.

"Don't trip, I'll get your damn pizza puff."

Another alert came through his phone, and he looked down at it, texting back.

"Don't worry about it, Black. I'm good. We're good."

He turned his attention back to her. "What the hell is that supposed to mean?"

"You're about to leave, right? You have some important case to see to, right?"

"Don't be like that; it's not good for the baby." He leaned in to give her a kiss, but she turned her face away.

"Just go, Black."

Black looked at Sapphire, reached into his pocket, and pulled out two hundred dollars. He handed the money to Sapphire. "Go and get your mama whatever she wants, and you keep the change. She's going to be too stubborn to take it herself."

Sapphire took the money, and Black turned and left as Stone stomped off to her room and slammed the door closed.

FIVE

O utside, Black's focus shifted to the text message he had just received. The number was unfamiliar, and the message contained a screenshot of a Bitcoin account bearing his name, holding a staggering $500,000. He scrutinized the image, desperately searching for any clues about its origin or legitimacy. When no answers emerged, he sent a text back, growing increasingly anxious with each passing second. When that yielded no response, he dialed the number, only to be sent to voicemail. A wave of frustration washed over Black. He longed for Seshat, his trusted hacker, but she had vanished after the Lagos incident, leaving him in the dark about her fate. Was she alive or dead? He had no way of knowing. His gaze shifted up the block, and he noticed a White Chevy Silverado. The man behind the wheel seemed to be watching him, or at least, that's what Black suspected. The stranger exited the truck and approached a nearby house. Instinctively, Black slid into his car and sped off.

As he raced down the highway toward Roseland to meet his father, he glanced in the rearview mirror and spotted the Silverado, mirroring his speed. Panic set in, and he decided to make a phone call. After exiting the highway, he glanced once more in the mirror, he saw the Silverado trailing him, a few blocks behind.

After a brief conversation on the phone, Black continued driving for another ten minutes before pulling over to the side of the road when he heard sirens approaching. He stayed put, watching carefully. Minutes later, he stepped out of his car and approached an unmarked police vehicle, exchanging a fist bump with the detective inside.

"I found a .38 and a handful of pills in his truck, a quick search showed he's on papers, paroled transferred in from Memphis, you got five minutes then I'm going to toss the gun and drugs and cut him loose. I had no real probable cause to stop him he's not worth the headache or paperwork."

"Thanks, Bunch, I owe you one."

Bunchy was a friend in the department, he worked in the missing children's department, when Black saw he was being followed, he called him in for backup, luckily, he wasn't too far away. Black slid into the front seat of Bunchy's car, his eyes fixed on the computer screen displaying information about Anthony Drake, a former inmate of FCI Memphis. Drake's criminal record was extensive. "Anthony Drake, formally of the FCI Memphis penitentiary, aggravated armed robbery, assault on a police officer, three counts of domestic violence, terroristic threats while brandishing a firearm, parole transferred to the great state of Illinois, now tell me Drakey, why would a piece of shit like you be in our city stinking up the place?"

"That stench was here long before I got to town, what the fuck is this, don't need to be an ex-con to see you ain't a cop."

"But you are...what are you following me for convict?"

"Who says I'm following you?" Drake shot back.

"I spotted you before I got on the highway, clear across town," Black replied, his tone unwavering.

"Coincidence," Drake mumbled.

"Who hired you?" Black pressed. Drake remained silent, prompting Black to continue, "Consider this a courtesy with my friend here stopping you. If I see you again, I won't be so courteous." Bunchy rapped on the car window, drawing Black's attention. Black looked up into the rearview mirror into the backseat at Drake, shook his head annoyingly, and got out of the car.

"He give you anything?" Bunchy asked.

Black shook his head, frustration etched on his face. "No, not a word. But trust me, we'll cross paths again, and he'll be more talkative next time, I guarantee it."

As Black walked back to his car, Bunchy opened the backdoor of his squad car and let Drake out, he uncuffed his hands. "You get a warning this time for the gun and drugs, that's a huge pass so I catch you so much as spit on the ground I'll make sure you're on the first thing smoking violated back to Memphis."

A smirk played across Drake's face. "Yes, sir officer."

Black watched as Drake got into his car, executed a U-turn, and drove in the opposite direction, his mind racing with unanswered questions about the mysterious Bitcoin account and the enigmatic Anthony Drake.

Six

Yehohanan stood on the sidewalk as the black Nissan Titan rolled up in front of him. The window slid down, and his heart skipped a beat when he heard that familiar voice.

"Yehohanan! It's me, Mandy!" Professor Moore shouted, yanking open the door, hopping inside, and slamming it shut. Their eyes locked, and their smiles stretched from ear to ear. "Man, I am so glad to see you!" she exclaimed.

"I'm glad to see you too," he replied, his gaze momentarily shifting to the cityscape outside as they began to move.

"All praises due," Professor Moore murmured, he didn't respond. She pressed on, the tension in the air evident. "What's the first thing you want to do, now that the Lord has brought you back home to us?"

Yehohanan let out a weary sigh. "The first thing I want to do is take a shower and have a long nap. I haven't slept for two days, for real." He chuckled. "You know, after a while, I learned to sleep like a baby behind those walls, sharing a room with different killers over the decades I was inside." He chuckled again. "But being on that bus, surrounded by regular everyday citizens, I tossed and turned all night."

"Why do you think that is?" Professor Moore inquired.

He shrugged. "Shit, I don't know. Maybe in there, I knew what I was dealing with, and respect was number one. Out here, it's less predictable. I don't know what someone might do."

She chuckled. "You make it sound as if the men you were inside with were honorable."

Yehohanan turned to face her. "Some were."

She cleared her throat. "Well, anyway, I know a lot has changed, and you have to process some things, so I'll give you your space."

"Thank you."

"Afterward, I'll take you shopping and get you some new clothes. I was thinking four or five outfits, two pairs of shoes, and a suit for church." Yehohanan cringed, and Professor Moore couldn't miss his reaction. She pressed on. "Is everything alright?"

"Listen, Mandy, I appreciate the gesture, but I'm going to pass on the church thing."

"Pass? Are you serious?" Her tone held a mix of surprise and concern. Yehohanan met her gaze, his expression stoic. She cleared her throat and continued, her voice gentle. "Why, what happened, Yehohanan? You were ordained as a teenager, as long as I've known you, you've always kept the Lord in your heart and walked by faith, steadfast to teach His word."

Yehohanan interrupted her. "It's safe to say you don't know me anymore, nor I you. I'm ready to get to know you again, and hopefully, you're willing to get to know me as I am now and not hold me to what I was."

Professor Moore fell silent, her hand finding its way to his leg, giving it a reassuring squeeze. He looked up and found her gazing at him with eyes devoid of judgment. She withdrew her hand and turned on the radio, and for the rest of the journey, they traveled in shared contemplative silence.

SEVEN

Back on the expressway hoping to finally make it to his father's without another distraction another text message came chiming through. He glanced down at his phone at another message from Deborah. A voice message he pressed the play button and listened.

"I don't even know why I'm calling you, because it's not like you give a fuck right?" There was a pause. Empty air filled the call, she continued. "Black, I'm so lost, I just found out my father passed away this morning. I have this case I'm supposed to testify in, and I don't know if I have the emotional headspace to do it. I don't know, I guess I just didn't want to be alone." She let out a sad laugh. "You know what, fuck it."

Black shook his head annoyed by the message, he pressed play and listened again, he wanted to see if he could sense a sign of manipulation in her tone. They hadn't been seeing one another long and he was the last person qualified to be anyone's emotional sounding board, yet she had done him a solid in the past he figured he would return the favor and pop up, he altered direction and headed towards Wicker Park.

***

The next morning, Black woke up with a pounding head, remnants of the previous night's revelry swirling in his thoughts. Surprisingly, the evening had gone smoother than he had expected. When he arrived at Deborah's place, she was already halfway through a bottle of Merlot. They had ordered food, indulged in a few more bottles of wine, and shared laughter and conversation. She had even shed a few tears, and, as the night wore on, they had both succumbed to exhaustion, falling asleep on the sofa in front of the television. Black lay there, his senses on high alert, listening for any sign of movement.

"Deborah!" he called out as he sat up. There was no response, only silence that seemed to hang heavily in the air. His gaze fell to his phone, revealing an unanswered text message from her.

"Morning love, had to run out early for court. Didn't want to wake you," the message read. "There's food and coffee in there if you need, left a key on the table, lock up. I'll be in late tonight, no pressure, but I'd love it if you're there when I get home."

Black's eyes shifted to the key resting on the table. He stood, picked it up, and headed to the kitchen. He opened the fridge and retrieved an apple, then opened the bread box, revealing a couple of muffins. Two of them found their way into his hand as he turned toward the door, fully intending to return home, shower, and change. But as he was about to step out, his phone rang. The number displayed was unfamiliar, and a hint of apprehension gripped him. Considering the mysterious Bitcoin account, he answered on the first ring.

"Hello," he said, his voice a touch cautious.

"Mr. Love," came the response from the other end.

"Yes," Black replied, his curiosity piqued.

"I am Assistant Principal Garcia at Latin School of Chicago. I'm calling about Johnny."

Black stepped out of Deborah's place, locking the door behind him. "Is everything alright?" he inquired, a growing sense of unease settling in.

"Unfortunately, no," Garcia responded gravely. "Johnny has been in a fight, and the other student has been injured severely. His parents are here, and I'm trying to get this resolved without involving the authorities. But I'm going to need you to come here and meet with the parents."

"I'm on my way," Black answered and promptly ended the call before Garcia could say anything further.

EIGHT

B lack made his way to the Gold Coast community where the school was located on the North Side. He parked in the visitor's parking space, hit the alarm on his car, and went inside. A staff member greeted him and, after he stated his business, escorted him to the principal's office. When Black walked in, the principal was sitting behind his desk. Johnny and the boy Johnny was accused of beating up sat next to each other. Standing in the back of the office, looking angrily at Johnny, were the boy's parents.

Black extended his hand to the principal, who took it in a firm shake. "So, what's going on here?" Black said, sliding his hands into his pockets.

"Well-" the principal began, but Black held up one hand, cutting him off.

"I'm not talking to you. I've heard your version of the story over the phone, that is unless you have more to add?"

Principal Garcia cleared his throat, pushed his glasses back on the bridge of his nose. "No, I do not," he responded, annoyed.

Black turned his attention to Johnny; Johnny raised his head and began speaking. "Whatever they said I did, I did."

"Don't be a smart ass. I can see from this kid's face you did what they say you did. I'm asking why?"

Johnny didn't respond; he shrugged his shoulders.

"Look at me," Black demanded. Johnny raised his head once more and locked eyes with Black. "Use your voice, boy."

"I don't know why I did it, sir. I just did it."

"That's not good enough."

"It's all I got, Black."

"We're pressing charges," the woman in the back of the room blurted out as she made her way towards the principal.

"And you are?" Black asked, looking past the woman to whom he assumed was her husband. The man reached his hand out to shake hands with Black. The woman stepped in front of him, cutting him off, locking eyes with Black.

"We are Mr. and Mrs. Rodriguez," she said with a hint of authority.

Black stared the woman down, not responding. She stared back, finally relenting and lowering her eyes. Her husband eased her to the side as he stepped forward, placing himself in front of her, and folded his arms across his chest. "I'm Timmy Rodriguez, Alderman of the 43rd ward."

"How do you want to handle this, Timmy, without getting the authorities involved?"

"I'm not sure that we can, Mr. Love."

"They're sixteen years old, a couple of boys fighting, it happens."

"This isn't the South Side, Mr. Love; we sent our son here to avoid situations like this."

Black turned and faced the principal. "Principal Garcia, there has to be another way. What about detention or in-school suspension?"

"I'm afraid it's out of my hands. The school superintendent has been cracking down on in-school violence with the recent wave of mass school shootings. They aren't taking any chances."

"Whoa, whoa, whoa, pump your brakes. This was two kids fighting. We're not going to label him the next Ethan Crumbley," Black said, referring to the mass school shooter a state over in Michigan. "I'll sue you, the Garcias, and the superintendent for slander."

"That's preposterous," Mrs. Rodriguez blurted out. "He's a menace, and he's going to jail."

"You might want to tell your wife to be quiet, Alderman. You two aren't the only ones who know people. I may no longer be District Attorney, but I still have more than a few people that owe me favors."

"Are you threatening me?" Mr. Rodriguez said as he stepped closer to Black.

"You're fucking right I'm threatening you."

"Let's everyone calm down. No one's suing anyone. This isn't going past the school. Since neither are saying what caused the fight, there's no way I can appoint blame to either."

Mrs. Rodriguez pushed past her husband and Black. She grabbed her son's face, who sat silently listening.

"You're a goddamn liar. You can't appoint blame. Look at my son's face!"

"That doesn't prove Johnny started the fight. It only proves he finished it. For all we know, there's a fifty percent chance your boy instigated it, and Johnny was only defending himself."

"Is that what happened, José?" His mother asked as she turned his face towards hers. He yanked away, folded his arms across his chest, and looked away.

"Johnny?" Principal Garcia asked. When Johnny didn't respond, Garcia continued. "Both will receive three days suspension and a month of detention. It will stay off of both of their records pending neither gets into any other trouble. If not, it goes in the file."

"Bullshit, we're still pressing charges," Mrs. Rodriguez stated matter-of-factly.

"That's fine, but I'm sure Mr. Love knows this already. Being an attorney, he has the right to do the same with your son. Both boys will be arrested, fingerprinted, and processed."

"Do you know who we are?" Mrs. Rodriguez said vehemently.

Black laughed. "Yes, I do. I know that me and the boy don't lose anything by being in the press or going viral, but Alderman, ask him how he feels about him and his son going viral?"

"You can't-"

"Ana! That's enough. José, let's go."

Black tapped Johnny on the shoulder, signaling it was time to go. He stood, locked eyes with José as the two groups left the principal's office.

As Black and Johnny stepped into the hallway, they paused, watching the Garcias walk toward the exit. The bell rang, and the hall swarmed with students, their chatter and footsteps filling the air.

Black's eyes scanned the crowd, always on alert. He noticed a kid with a black eye moving past. The kid caught Johnny's gaze, hesitated, then hurried along after Johnny gave him a nod and a wink.

"Hold up," Black muttered, pulling out his phone. He pretended to scroll through messages, his body turned just enough to keep the kid in his peripheral vision. With a quick flick of his thumb, he snapped a covert picture, using the pretense of typing to keep it discreet. No one noticed.

He slid the phone back into his pocket, his expression giving nothing away. "Alright, let's go," he said, nodding at Johnny. They headed for the exit, stepping into the crisp spring air, the weight of the situation lingering as the sounds of the city swirled around them.

NINE

"So, this is where you live?" Yehohanan asked as Professor Moore turned the corner onto her daughter's block.

"No, this is where Angie lives," she replied, slowing down as she looked for a place to park. Suddenly, she spotted Sheek Green emerging from the building. Quickly, she turned her head, hoping not to be seen, and continued driving.

"Wow, I finally get to meet Angie. I've watched her grow up through pictures and letters," he said, glancing through his rearview mirror and noticing that she wasn't stopping. "What's wrong? I thought we were stopping at Angie's?"

She feigned a smile. "Nothing's wrong. I just remembered I needed to get to the house first. We'll stop by Angie's later." She drove for another three blocks before pulling over to the side of the road. "I need to make a private phone call. Give me a minute." Before he could respond, she hopped out of the car and closed the door behind her.

Yehohanan watched through his passenger door mirror as Professor Moore paced back and forth, speaking animatedly into her phone. He couldn't hear her words, but her tense body language and the way she kept glancing around made him uneasy. After a few minutes, she hung up and made another call, this one shorter than the first. She climbed back into the car and started the engine without a word.

"You sure everything is alright, Mandy?" he asked, concern evident in his voice.

"Yeah, I'm good," she replied curtly.

Yehohanan didn't push the issue, but he could feel that everything was definitely not good. The atmosphere in the car was thick with unspoken tension. He glanced at her, noting the tight grip she had on the steering wheel and the way her eyes darted nervously between the road and the rearview mirror.

As they drove in silence, Yehohanan's mind raced. He had known Mandy for years and could tell when something was off. The detour, the hurried phone calls, and her evasive behavior all pointed to something serious. But what?

"Is there anything I can do to help?" he asked gently, trying to bridge the gap that had suddenly formed between them.

She shook her head, her lips pressed into a thin line. "No, it's just some work stuff. Nothing you need to worry about."

Yehohanan wasn't convinced, but he respected her need for privacy. He leaned back in his seat, staring out the window as they continued driving. The cityscape blurred past them, but his mind was fixed on the mystery that seemed to be unraveling around them.

After a few more minutes of silence, Mandy's phone buzzed. She glanced at the screen, her face paling as she read the message. She quickly shoved the phone back into her bag and tightened her grip on the wheel.

"Are you sure you're okay, Mandy?" Yehohanan asked again, more insistently this time.

She nodded, but her eyes betrayed her. "Yeah, I'm fine. Let's just get home. We'll go see Angie later, I promise."

Yehohanan nodded, but he couldn't shake the feeling that something was very wrong. As they drove through the city, he silently vowed to find out what was going on and help Mandy in any way he could.

TEN

The Escalade sat idling near the curb, its engine a low, constant hum. Sheek's driver sat silently behind the wheel, fingers drumming against the leather steering wheel, his eyes scanning the street ahead. A few stragglers wandered the sidewalks, huddled under umbrellas or clutching their coats tight against the wind. The air smelled of wet asphalt and the faint aroma of hot dogs from a cart a block away. The driver shifted in his seat, stealing a glance at Sheek through the rearview mirror.

"It's gonna rain again," the driver muttered, his voice cutting through the sound of the windshield wipers lazily flicking back and forth. "Spring don't know if it wants to stick around or keep messing with winter."

Sheek didn't respond at first, taking a slow drag on his cigarette and watching the smoke dance in front of the window. His eyes followed the movements of the pedestrians outside, his mind working but his body still as stone. The city felt like it was waiting for something. He flicked the ash from his cigarette out the cracked window and turned his head slightly.

"Chicago's always playing games with the weather, the city is kind of like the people in it ain't it?" Sheek said finally, his voice low and gravelly.

"How's that?"

"Never know what you're gonna get, and it'll switch on you before you can adjust."

Ringing from Sheek's phone cut the conversation short as he answered on the first ring. He listened more than he spoke before ending the call. It wasn't quite what he wanted to hear, but it was a start.

"You heard from Drake?" He asked his driver as he placed a cigarette in his mouth and lit it.

"Nah, he's still following the P.I."

"Get him on the phone, tell him check in at the bar."

"On it boss, what's the play?"

"She wants to meet."

The driver looked up, hesitating. "What about her kid? When she finds out—"

"That's why she's not going to find out. Clean it up—take her phone, take her bag. Dump them across state lines. Keep the GPS live till it pings in Ohio." Sheek took a drag of his cigarette, a shadow crossing his mind—a thought of his own daughter, long estranged. He flicked the ash away. This wasn't the time.

The driver did as he was told and pulled off.

ELEVEN

Black and Johnny sat in the car, the hum of the engine steady as they drove away from the school. The city rolled by in flashes—tall buildings, traffic lights, the occasional horn blaring—while inside the car, there was nothing but heavy silence. Black's hands gripped the steering wheel, his jaw tight. Johnny stared out the window, his face blank, but the tension between them was thick, hanging in the air like smoke.

After a few minutes of quiet, Black spoke, his voice low and controlled. "You wanna tell me why it happened?"

Johnny didn't look away from the window. "No."

Black shot him a quick glance, his eyes narrowing. "That's not gonna work with me, Johnny. You know that."

Johnny shifted in his seat but still didn't turn. "It just... did."

Black exhaled through his nose, his grip tightening on the wheel. "So you just decided to swing on a kid, no reason?"

Johnny didn't answer right away. "He was talking."

"Talking?" Black echoed, his voice edged with disbelief. "So you laid him out for talking?"

Johnny shrugged, his tone flat. "Yeah."

The car rolled to a stop at a red light, and Black took the opportunity to look at Johnny, studying his face. "You started it, didn't you?"

This time, Johnny finally turned his head to meet Black's gaze, his expression unreadable but his eyes holding a flicker of something—guilt, maybe. "Yeah."

Black nodded slowly, turning back to the road as the light changed and they moved forward. "Why?"

Johnny stayed quiet, his lips pressed together in a thin line.

"Look," Black continued, his tone firm but calm. "I get it. Sometimes people say things, push you, make you feel like you gotta react. But you don't just get to walk around hitting people, no matter what they say. So I'm asking again—why?"

Johnny didn't answer right away, his face tightening like he was chewing on the words. "He deserved it."

Black's eyes flicked toward Johnny, catching the hardness in his voice. He sighed. "You think beating him up solves anything?"

"No."

"You think it makes you right?"

"No."

"So why do it?"

Johnny shrugged again, staring down at his hands. "It's all I had at the time."

Black nodded, letting the words hang for a moment. He wasn't going to push Johnny into saying more than he wanted, but he wasn't going to let this slide, either.

"Alright," Black said, his voice steady. "Here's what's gonna happen. I'm gonna take some time to figure out what your punishment's gonna be."

Johnny didn't react, but his body stiffened slightly in his seat.

"You're gonna be punished, don't doubt that. But I'm gonna make sure it fits. And it's gonna be something that sticks. Understand?"

Johnny gave a small nod, his eyes still fixed on the passing city. "Yeah."

Black glanced at him again, a little softer this time. "Good. Now sit tight, and don't make this a habit."

The silence returned, but this time it felt different. The tension had eased, leaving behind something unspoken but understood. As they drove through the streets of Chicago, Black kept his eyes on the road, but his mind was already turning over the options for how to handle Johnny's mess.

Punishment wasn't just about consequence. It was about making sure Johnny understood—really understood—that there were other ways to fight back, other ways to deal with the shit life threw at you. Black wasn't going to let him spiral. Not on his watch.

TWELVE

B lack pulled up in front of his office, tapped the horn, and waited. A moment later, Joanne stepped onto the porch. He rolled down Johnny's window and called out, "Joanne, come here real quick."

He rolled the window back up, turning to Johnny. "Stick close until we talk. Don't make it hard for me to find you."

"Yes sir." Johnny got out, smirking as he passed Joanne. Black rolled the window down as she leaned in.

"What's up?" she asked.

Without looking up from his phone, Black sent a quick text. Her phone buzzed, and she glanced at the message. "I just sent you a photo of a kid from Johnny's school. Find out who he is and what his relationship with Johnny is. Keep this between us."

Joanne hesitated, but nodded. "Got it, boss. I'll let you know."

As she stepped away, Black pulled off without another word.

THIRTEEN

Black's phone buzzed again, the number flashing like a dare. This time, no cryptic taunts. Just an address. His gut twisted, a familiar unease curling in his chest. He forwarded the message to Sloane Kincaid, the only person he trusted in moments like this. She always stayed hidden until it mattered.

Got it, she texted back, short and efficient.

They made a quick stop before heading to Rock Island. Black changed into fresh clothes—nothing flashy, just enough to blend in. He didn't need attention here, not in Sheek's territory. The bar was notorious—dim, heavy with the scent of stale beer and desperation. The kind of place where you could get lost without trying.

Sloane slipped in first, moving like smoke. She positioned herself in the back, unnoticed, eyes sharp. She was invisible until she wasn't, her presence a safety net Black wouldn't call unless absolutely necessary.

Black entered a few minutes later, the weight of tension thick in the air. He scanned the room—sizing it up. Low murmurs, clinking glasses, shadows playing tricks in the dim light. At a table near the back, Professor Moore sat, calm, composed. Beside her, Yehohanan loomed—a hulking figure, silent but watchful. The prison garb was gone, but the man didn't need it to make a statement. His presence did the talking, his eyes tracking every move.

To the untrained eye, Black and Yehohanan might've seemed like Moore's muscle. But Black knew better. This wasn't her show. Not anymore.

Sheek emerged from the shadows, his smile sharp and cold. The type that didn't quite reach his eyes. He moved like a man who enjoyed watching people squirm.

"Well, well," Sheek's voice slid through the air, smooth as oil. "Didn't think you had the guts to show."

Black's eyes flickered, the tension rippling beneath his calm. His fingers brushed the weight of the gun at his side, a quiet reminder. He relaxed his grip, choosing words over war. For now.

"I'm not hiding. No reason to." His voice was steady, deliberate.

Sheek's smile twitched, a darker edge creeping in. His gaze lingered on Moore before locking back on Black.

"You know why we're here. Professor Moore wants her daughter, but that's not happening until I get what's mine. All of it."

The air shifted, heavy with threat. Black could feel Sheek's eyes drilling into him, searching for a crack, a weakness. He wouldn't find one.

"I've been getting texts," Sheek continued, his voice cutting through the tension like a blade. "Text after text, saying you've got my money. Half a mil. Bitcoin. You think this is a game?"

Black's jaw tightened. He was being played—puppeteered into the center of someone's twisted scheme. He didn't like it. But guilty or not, he was stuck in this web, and Sheek wasn't planning to let him crawl out clean.

"I don't have your money," Black said, his voice low, controlled. "But you're not going to use her daughter as a bargaining chip. You'll get your money. Just don't pull the wrong strings."

Sheek leaned in, his smile snaking back onto his face, sharp and dangerous. "Oh, you'll get me my money, alright. Or her daughter's gone for good."

The words hung between them like a noose, pulling tighter with each second of silence. Black's mind worked fast, calculating the angles. Sloane was somewhere in the shadows, watching, ready to act if needed. But for now, it was a game of words, and Sheek was holding the cards.

Black glanced at Professor Moore. She didn't flinch, didn't move. She had pulled them all into this room, but she wasn't in control of the endgame. He was.

Sheek sat back, his eyes never leaving Black. "Clock's ticking, Love. Get me my money."

The bar grew quieter, the tension thick enough to choke on. Black leaned back in his chair, sizing up the situation, knowing whatever move came next would set the course for everything that followed.

Out of the corner of his eye, Black caught a subtle exchange—Anthony Drake, sitting in the shadows, nodding at him. The recognition was quiet, but there. Black met Drake's gaze briefly, then dismissed it, filing it away. But before he could turn back, he caught something else. A glance. A flicker of the eyes between Drake and Moore. It was quick, a passing signal. Something unspoken.

Black blinked. The pieces shifted. There was something else here, something deeper. He wasn't sure what, but he'd figure it out. For now, though, all that mattered was the clock ticking down—and keeping his next move sharp.

He leaned forward, eyes locked on Sheek. "You'll get what you deserve, Sheek. Trust me on that."

The room stayed thick with tension, the kind that only broke when someone was left standing—or bleeding.

Black pulled up in front of his office, tapped the horn, and waited. A moment later, Joanne stepped onto the porch. He rolled down Johnny's window and called out, "Joanne, come here real quick."

He rolled the window back up, turning to Johnny. "Stick close until we talk. Don't make it hard for me to find you."

"Yes sir." Johnny got out, smirking as he passed Joanne. Black rolled the window down as she leaned in.

"What's up?" she asked.

Without looking up from his phone, Black sent a quick text. Her phone buzzed, and she glanced at the message. "I just sent you a photo of a kid from Johnny's school. Find out who he is and what his relationship with Johnny is. Keep this between us."

Joanne hesitated, but nodded. "Got it, boss. I'll let you know."

As she stepped away, Black pulled off without another word.

FOURTEEN

A s the tension in the room pulled tight like a noose, Black's phone buzzed in his pocket. He glanced down, sending a quick, discreet text to Sloane:

"Follow Drake. Black dude, late thirties. Short dreads, scar under his left eye. Don't lose him."

The reply came just as fast:

"On it."

The bar was steeped in shadows, low lights barely illuminating faces clouded with menace. The group rose from their seats, the atmosphere charged with unspoken threats. Black's eyes flicked to Professor Moore, her face a mask of icy control, the kind of woman who always had an angle—always a move planned ahead of time. Beside her, Yehohanan loomed, the silent giant, his hulking frame casting an even darker shadow. He was like a loaded gun, always in the room but never firing. But Black knew the truth—guns don't stay silent forever.

Once they stepped outside, the crisp night air felt suffocating, thick with the weight of everything unsaid. Black turned on his heel, confronting Professor Moore. His voice was low, quiet—dangerous.

"You roped me into this mess, Moore. I told you, I'm out. But here I am, knee-deep in your shit. I warned you."

She didn't blink, her eyes gleaming under the streetlight, sharp as razors. With a smirk that was equal parts sarcasm and venom, she said, "What's the problem, Black? Want your five grand now? You earned it."

Black's jaw tightened, the anger seething beneath the surface. "I don't want your dirty money. What I want is answers." He leaned in, voice colder than the night air. "What's the key code for the Bitcoin account? You said you needed to pay Sheek his money, so don't act like you don't know."

Moore met his gaze without flinching, her smirk barely fading. "I don't know the code."

Black's face darkened, his patience wearing thin. He took another step closer, towering over her, the air between them crackling with tension. "You better be telling the truth," He hissed, "because if you're not, we're all on borrowed time."

Yehohanan watched from a step away, his face blank, the unreadable kind of stillness that made him feel more like a shadow than a man. Even in silence, his presence was oppressive, like he was always one breath away from violence.

Black glanced at him, his words barely a mutter. "You've got nothing to say, huh?" Yehohanan's eyes flickered, but he didn't move, didn't speak. Just stood there, a hulking reminder that there was no way out without getting your hands bloody.

Moore stepped forward, brushing past Black, her voice as cold as her gaze. "Always the dramatic one, Black. We've got forty-eight hours to get Sheek his money. After that, we're all dead." Her words hung in the air, the finality of them twisting the tension into a noose around their necks. "We'll meet at my place. Make sure you're there. Unless you want Sheek to come looking for you."

Black stood there for a second, letting her words settle in. Twenty-four hours. The clock had started ticking. He cast one last look at Moore and Yehohanan before turning away, his mind already working, calculating. This wasn't just a game anymore—it was survival.

They moved together down the darkened street, an unlikely trio bound by necessity. The streets were quieter now, but the danger was ever-present, lurking just out of sight. It felt like Chicago itself was watching, the city's shadows stretching long under the dim streetlights, following them to wherever this dark road led.

The night had turned into something darker, more sinister. And Black, once just a player in someone else's game, was now one of the pieces being moved across the board. But there was something none of them knew yet—Black didn't play by the rules. Not anymore.

FIFTEEN

J oanne scrolled through Snapchat, her thumb pausing as she found his profile—the boy from Johnny's school. She had followed him almost right after Black had sent her the photo, she plugged it into Google search and found his social media profile, playing her role, liking his stories, and sending casual comments. It didn't take long before he responded, his awkward attempts at flirting making her smile. She was good at this, knew how to make someone feel seen, make them want to share.

She leaned back in her chair, her fingers moving quickly across the screen, setting up a meeting.

"Let's grab coffee. Gold Coast. Corner of Dearborn and Goethe. 4 pm. You game?"

He was hesitant at first, but within minutes, his reply came through.

"Yeah, sure! See you there."

When Joanne arrived at the corner, she spotted him immediately—nervous, jittery, and way out of his comfort zone. He looked like the kind of kid who had probably never been on a date with a girl like her. She smiled inwardly. It wasn't about attraction, though. This was about getting information.

As she approached him, his eyes widened, and he fumbled with his phone, almost dropping it. He stood up awkwardly, a grin plastered across his face.

"Hey... wow, you actually came," he said, his voice shaky. He tried to make small talk, nervously complimenting her shoes, her hair, anything to fill the silence.

Joanne wasn't here for games, though. She got straight to the point, sliding into the chair across from him. "So, what happened to your face?"

The question landed like a punch. He froze for a moment, looking around as if the busy street could somehow offer an escape. He hadn't expected her to be this direct.

"Uh, what do you mean?" he stammered, shifting in his seat, his hand automatically moving to his cheek as if remembering the bruise.

She leaned forward slightly, her fingers brushing his hand. "You know exactly what I mean," she said softly, her voice calm but firm. "Who did that to you?"

He hesitated, eyes darting away. But then, her touch seemed to relax him, his shoulders slumping as he let out a breath he didn't realize he was holding. The tension in him melted, and the words came easier.

"It was... it was that Garcia kid," he mumbled. "You know, the Alderman's son? He's been giving me a hard time since the start of the school year. I'm, like, one of the only Black kids at the school, and he won't let me forget it."

Joanne listened, her expression soft but focused. She knew this would get messy.

"He said I was a 'nepo baby,' that I didn't belong there. That my parents just bought me in," he continued, his voice barely above a whisper. "I was getting beat up in the hallways, harassed online. It got so bad I didn't want to go to school anymore."

"How come you didn't fight back?" she asked, her voice softer this time but still direct.

He hesitated, chewing on his lip. His shoulders hunched as if he were trying to make himself smaller. "Honestly?" he whispered, barely looking at her. "I was scared. I didn't know what to do…"

Joanne tilted her head, watching him carefully, waiting for him to open up.

He took a deep breath, finally letting the words spill out. "But this other kid… he stepped in. Out of nowhere." His voice picked up a little, like he was reliving the moment. "He didn't care what was happening or who they were. He just… helped me."

She raised an eyebrow, playing ignorant. "Oh really? Who was that?"

The boy's face brightened, some of the tension draining out of him. He leaned in a little closer, the excitement bubbling up. "Johnny. His name's Johnny."

She kept her expression neutral, though inside, she felt a flicker of pride.

"Garcia had been giving me shit for months. Just 'cause I'm one of the few Black kids at school, y'know?" He swallowed hard, his voice low. "Calling me a 'nepo baby,' saying I didn't belong there. He had his crew with him, and they'd been pushing me around. I didn't know what to do. And then… Johnny."

His eyes lit up as he continued. "Johnny didn't even hesitate. Just went right at them. He took down two of them before they knew what was happening. The rest backed off real quick after that."

The boy grinned, clearly still in awe. "He's a badass. Ever since that day, no one's messed with me. It's like Johnny's some kind of legend at school now. They all talk about him."

Joanne listened, keeping her face calm, but inside, she felt that pride swell. Johnny had stood up, not just for himself, but for this kid too.

She glanced at her phone, pretending to check the time. "Thanks for sharing that," she said, standing up from the table. "I appreciate it."

The boy looked up at her, clearly not ready for the conversation to end. "Oh, yeah... no problem."

Joanne leaned down and kissed him on the cheek, her voice soft but final. "Take care of yourself."

With that, she turned and walked away, blending into the crowd. The city streets hummed around her, but inside, all she could think about was Johnny. He had done the right thing, and it made her proud in a way she hadn't expected. But there was more to this. She knew it. There was always more.

SIXTEEN

S loane followed Anthony Drake through the streets of Chicago, her car two lengths behind his black sedan. She had been tailing him for over an hour now, watching as he made several unremarkable stops—cheap diners, liquor stores, a pawn shop—each one more nondescript than the last. But she kept her distance, patient. Drake was clearly making moves, and she needed to see where they led.

It was well past midnight when Drake pulled onto the 4600 block of West Monroe Street. The neighborhood was quiet, the kind of place that had gone to sleep hours ago, except for a few scattered figures lingering in the shadows. Sloane parked a block away, moving silently on foot. She watched as Drake approached what looked like an old, run-down building with a brightly lit sign that read *"All-Star Kids 24-Hour Daycare."*

She blinked. A daycare? At this hour?

Something wasn't right. Drake walked past the chain-link fence and into the alley, disappearing into the back entrance. Sloane slipped in after him, her eyes scanning for cameras, her footsteps as silent as a whisper on the cracked concrete. She rounded the corner just in time to see Drake knock on an unmarked steel door behind the daycare. A thick-necked man with tattooed arms opened it, giving Drake a quick once-over before letting him in.

Sloane knew she had to be careful now. She waited, hidden in the shadows, watching as the door closed behind Drake. After a few minutes, she approached, checking her surroundings before slipping into the alley. The daycare was just a front, she realized. Whatever was happening here had nothing to do with taking care of kids.

She knocked twice, mimicking the rhythm Drake had used. The door opened, and she held her breath, her face hidden beneath the brim of her cap. She nodded to the bouncer, playing the part of someone who belonged. To her relief, he let her through without question.

Inside, the atmosphere shifted immediately. What had appeared to be a dilapidated daycare on the outside gave way to something far more upscale and sinister below. The narrow stairwell led to a large, low-ceilinged basement—a hidden club filled with dim lights, velvet booths, and smoke swirling from cigars. The air was heavy with the smell of expensive alcohol and quiet tension, the kind of place where people did business you never wrote down. Music thumped low in the background, creating a subtle, ominous beat.

Sloane kept to the shadows, slipping into the back corner where the light barely reached. From her position, she had a full view of the room. Drake was already at the bar, a drink in hand, but he wasn't there to unwind. He was waiting for someone. She glanced around, searching for clues.

Then she saw him.

A man entered from a back room—a tall, silver-haired figure dressed in a sharp suit that screamed money and power. He moved with purpose, making a beeline for Drake. They exchanged a quick handshake, their conversation too quiet to hear over the music. Sloane slipped her phone out, pretending to check messages, but really using the front-facing camera to snap photos of the interaction.

She leaned in closer, careful not to draw attention. From what she could gather, Drake wasn't here for a social visit. The silver-haired man slid a briefcase across the bar to Drake, who opened it quickly, his eyes scanning the contents. Sloane couldn't see inside, but the look on Drake's face told her all she needed to know—whatever was in that case, it was important.

She focused on their body language, the subtle tension between them. This wasn't a transaction between equals. Drake was clearly working for this guy—or worse, he was in over his head.

As the conversation went on, Sloane caught snippets of their exchange.

"...this better be enough," Drake muttered, his voice strained but low.

The man in the suit didn't even flinch. "It'll keep him off your back for now. But you'd better finish what you started. The money's only a Band-Aid."

Sloane's heart raced. She was piecing it together. This wasn't just about Sheek and Black's money. Drake was playing his own game, and it was clear he was in deeper than anyone knew.

Suddenly, the silver-haired man leaned in, his voice dropping lower. "Don't think I didn't hear about your little Bitcoin stunt. You're lucky I don't have time to deal with your bullshit right now."

Drake clenched his jaw but said nothing, shoving the briefcase closed.

Sloane stayed hidden, her mind racing. The pieces were falling into place, but the picture wasn't clear yet. One thing was certain—Drake was moving money, likely Sheek's, but this briefcase exchange pointed to something bigger. He wasn't just an errand boy. He had his own motives, and this Bitcoin play was at the center of it.

Sloane took one last glance at Drake, her phone buzzing softly in her pocket. It was Black.

"You get anything yet?"

She slipped out of the club the same way she came in, her pulse steady but her mind buzzing with possibilities. Drake had no idea what was coming, and soon, Black would have the upper hand. But for now, she kept quiet, ready to follow the next thread of the web Drake was weaving.

The game had just gotten a whole lot more dangerous.

SEVENTEEN

B lack paced outside Professor Moore's apartment building, the shadows of the streetlights slicing through the dark like knives. His patience was gone, shredded by the weight of secrets he couldn't unravel.

"You ready to talk yet?" he asked, his voice sharp, cutting through the night air.

Professor Moore leaned against her car, arms crossed, her eyes cold, calculating. She wasn't rattled—never rattled. "You don't need to know everything, Black. Just enough to get the job done."

"That's the problem," Black shot back, his frustration boiling over. "You've got me tangled up in this mess, but you won't even give me the full story. You think I'm gonna stick my neck out for you when you won't come clean?"

Moore didn't flinch. "I already told you. Focus on Sheek. My daughter's life is on the line."

"And what about mine?" Black stepped closer, his eyes locked on hers. "I don't even know your daughter. Hell, I just met you. So why should I care if you're not gonna be upfront with me?"

She was silent, her jaw tight. Black shook his head, the disgust clear on his face.

"Screw this," he muttered, turning on his heel. "I'll handle Sheek my way. To hell with your daughter."

He started walking off, his steps heavy, determined. He didn't owe these people a damn thing.

Yehohanan, the silent giant, peeled away from the shadows. He lumbered after Black, his movements slow but deliberate. "Wait," he called out, his voice a low rumble.

Black kept walking, but Yehohanan quickened his pace, catching up. "I don't know the whole story either, man. But Mandy's good peoples. She needs help."

Black stopped, turning to face him. His eyes were sharp, cutting through Yehohanan's quiet demeanor. "I just met her yesterday. Now my life's on the line for someone I don't know? Her daughter's missing, I'm caught in the middle, and now I've got some old white dude covered in tattoos trying to convince me to throw it all away? Who the hell are you? And what's she got on you?"

Yehohanan just stared, his face blank, unreadable. "Keeping it real," he said slowly, "she probably owes me. But I don't care about that."

Black raised an eyebrow, waiting.

Yehohanan took a deep breath, his eyes darkening with memories. "Fifty-five years ago, I was just a kid. Fifteen. Southside. Civil Rights Movement was tearing the city apart. I wasn't part of it—just a scared white boy. One night, I saw these men corner a girl in an alley. Amanda. She was pregnant. Black. Didn't do nothing but be in the wrong place. They were gonna hurt her. I grabbed a pipe—only thing I could find—and I swung. Didn't stop swinging until one of them was dead."

He paused, his voice heavy with the weight of the past. "I saved two lives that night. Hers and her baby's."

Black stared at him, his face unreadable. "And threw yours in the trash."

Yehohanan nodded slowly. "That's all perspective."

"How long you been home?" Black asked, his tone flat, as if already knowing the answer.

"Day," Yehohanan replied, his eyes distant.

Black let out a low chuckle, shaking his head. "A day, huh? Man, if I were you, I'd walk away from her before she takes what scraps of life you've got left."

Yehohanan didn't say a word, just stared at Black with eyes that carried decades of loss. Pleading. Desperate.

Black held his gaze for a moment, then threw his hands up. "Good luck, man," he muttered, turning away.

Behind him, Professor Moore's voice sliced through the night, sharp and bitter. "Screw him! We don't need him!"

Black didn't turn around, didn't acknowledge her. He just kept walking, the city swallowing him whole, his shadow stretching long under the streetlights.

EIGHTEEN

B lack gripped the steering wheel, his thoughts a storm of frustration and anger. The night had gone sideways, and now he was just trying to hold it all together. His phone buzzed in the console, and for a moment, he thought about ignoring it. Probably Sloane or more trouble creeping in. But something made him glance at the screen.

Stone's face flashed across it.

He answered on the first ring, his instincts kicking in. "What's up?" His voice was sharper than he intended, still wound up from the confrontation with Professor Moore.

But it wasn't Stone's voice on the other end. It was Sapphire, her tone shaky, scared. "Black, it's me. Mama's in the hospital."

His grip tightened on the wheel, his pulse spiking. "What happened?" His voice dropped, now serious, the anger gone in an instant.

"She collapsed. I'm at Advocate in Palos Hills. Please hurry, Black. I'm really scared."

The line went dead before he could ask anything else. A wave of dread swept over him, hot and suffocating. Without a second thought, he gunned the engine and peeled out, tires screeching as the car shot forward. His mind raced with thoughts of Stone—the baby—how everything had just taken a sharp, terrifying turn. He didn't even bother with the GPS. He knew where the hospital was, and he sure as hell wasn't going to take his time getting there.

The streets were a blur as he sped through intersections, barely slowing for red lights, weaving through traffic like a man on a mission. Anger simmered low in his gut, but fear kept it in check. Black didn't scare easy, but this? This had him on edge. Stone wasn't just another woman in his life, and now, with the baby involved, everything had shifted.

Every second felt like an eternity as he pushed the car harder, the engine roaring in protest. Palos Hills wasn't far, but tonight, it felt like the longest drive of his life.

By the time he screeched into the hospital parking lot, his nerves were strung tight. He killed the engine and practically jumped out, heading straight for the doors, the cold night air biting at him, but he didn't feel it.

As soon as he stepped into the waiting room, he spotted Saphire talking to a doctor. She looked small, vulnerable, her usual confidence replaced with worry. Black strode over, heart still pounding, his eyes darting between Saphire and the doctor.

"I'm Black," he said, his voice clipped, still breathless from the drive. "What's going on with Stone?"

The doctor, a calm-looking man with graying hair, nodded. "Mr. Love, your wife has a condition called preeclampsia. It can be fatal if not treated, but we caught it in time. She's stable now."

Black's heart skipped a beat, but he kept his face steady. "When can we take her home?"

"We'd like to keep her overnight for observation. She should be able to go home in the morning, but she'll need to be on strict bed rest."

Black nodded, trying to steady his breathing. "And the baby?"

The doctor offered a small smile, the kind meant to reassure. "As far as we can tell, the baby's fine. But we'll be keeping a close watch."

Black let out a breath he hadn't realized he was holding. "Can I see her?"

"Of course," the doctor said. "But try not to stay too long. She needs her rest."

Black nodded his thanks and turned to Saphire. Together, they walked down the hall toward Stone's room, the sterile smell of the hospital pressing down on them.

Saphire stepped in first, moving to her mother's side. Black hung back, watching as the two shared a quiet moment. He saw the relief in Saphire's face as she gently touched Stone's hand, her whispered words too soft for him to hear. After a moment, Saphire turned to him, nodding before she quietly stepped out of the room, leaving the door cracked behind her.

Black walked in, his footsteps soft on the tile floor. Stone lay there, pale but alert, her eyes tracking him as he approached. There was a flicker of something in her gaze—relief, maybe, or something sharper. Stone's lips curled into a faint smile, her voice softer than usual. Then her smile faded slightly, her hand resting on her swollen belly. "Guess I scared you, huh?"

"Scared? Hell, I thought I was gonna lose you." Black's voice was rougher than usual, the weight of his fear leaking through. He leaned forward, his hand resting on hers. "I thought... you and the baby..."

"We're fine," Stone whispered, her eyes softening. "We're okay."

Black swallowed hard, leaning back in the chair. "I'm gonna do better by you. By both of you. No more bullshit. When you leave here, I'm gonna make sure you're taken care of."

Stone's gaze searched his, her skepticism clear, but there was a glimmer of hope there too. "Is that right?"

"Yeah, that's right," Black said firmly. "No more half-assing it. I'm all in."

For a moment, it felt like they were on the same page, like maybe, just maybe, things would be okay. But then Black's phone buzzed again, the sound cutting through the fragile peace between them. He glanced at the screen—Sloane. He ignored it, turning his attention back to Stone.

She saw it, though, her eyes narrowing. "Answer it."

"It's nothing," Black said, brushing it off. "Not now."

"Answer it," she repeated, her voice sharp, leaving no room for argument.

With a sigh, Black picked up the phone, pressing it to his ear. "What's up?"

"I want to meet," Sloane's voice came through, tense. "We need to talk."

Black glanced at Stone, hesitation pulling at him. "Now?"

"Yes. It's important."

Black sighed, running a hand across his bald head. "Fine. Where?"

"I'll send the location."

Black hung up, turning back to Stone, his expression conflicted. "I'll be back. I just need to—"

Stone's lips curled into a bitter smile. "Go," Stone said, cutting him off. "But if you're not here in the morning, don't bother coming to the house at all."

"Stone, c'mon, it's not like that," Black started, but she shook her head, cutting him off again.

"Don't. Just go." Her voice was cold now, the warmth from earlier evaporated.

Black stood there, torn, wanting to say more, to explain, but knowing it wouldn't change anything. He stared at her for a moment longer before turning and walking out, his shoulders heavy with the weight of her words.

The door clicked softly behind him. As he stepped into the hallway, he saw Saphire standing there, her back against the wall, her phone pressed to her ear. She glanced at him, her face unreadable, then turned away, her voice low as she spoke into the phone.

Black didn't linger. He walked in the opposite direction, the walls of the hospital closing in on him. His mind was already on the next move, the next problem. But Stone's words clung to him, heavy and suffocating.

NINETEEN

Black pulled up behind the dusty, black-on-black 2024 Rivian, the newness of the truck dulled by the layer of grime clinging to it. He parked, got out, and slid into the passenger seat next to Sloane. She sat behind the wheel, her fingers drumming lightly on the dashboard. No greeting, no small talk.

"What are we doing here?" he asked, his eyes flicking across the street to the Langham Hotel.

Sloane pointed. "Recognize the truck?"

Black squinted, shrugged. "Drake's."

"Yeah. And that car down the block?"

He looked, recognizing the sleek form of Professor Moore's car. "The professor," he said, matter-of-fact.

Sloane nodded, watching his face. "She pulled up after Drake. The white boy with her?"

"Nah. Just her. What's the deal with him?"

"Long story."

"They in on this together? Her and Drake?"

"Looks that way."

Black glanced at her, eyes narrowing. "What's the play?"

Sloane leaned back in her seat, her eyes never leaving the hotel. "I'm waiting. You're going home."

"You sure?"

"Yeah. Thanks." She held out her fist.

Black bumped it, then slipped out of the truck, crossing the street back to his car. He slid into the driver's seat, leaned back, and turned the music up. For thirty minutes, he waited, the tension winding tighter with each passing minute. His eyes stayed glued to the Langham's entrance, and finally, Professor Moore emerged, slipping into her car like a ghost in the night.

Black followed, keeping his distance as she wound through the city, back to her building. She parked, got out, and disappeared inside. Black lingered, waiting just long enough to watch her go, before stepping out and trailing her. The security door buzzed as someone exited, and he slipped in without a second thought. His eyes darted around the lobby as he pulled out his phone and dialed her number.

A faint ringtone echoed from the third floor.

He hung up before she could answer and headed up the stairwell, his footsteps silent on the cold concrete. When he reached the third floor, it was empty, quiet except for the distant hum of a broken light flickering above him. He dialed again, moving slowly down the hall, his ear to the apartment doors as he passed, waiting for the sound to betray her.

Halfway down the hall, he stopped. A phone was ringing behind a door that stood slightly ajar.

He pushed the door open, not stepping in but standing just outside, his body still in the shadows. The voices inside grew louder—sharp, agitated. A man and a woman.

Black leaned against the doorframe, his eyes cutting through the dim light of the apartment. Professor Moore stood over a man on the floor, the same dead man she'd stashed in her closet. The knife was still jutting out of his chest, but now, Yehohanan hovered over the body, silent as ever.

Moore's eyes flicked up, locking on Black. "You really don't know when to leave well enough alone, do you?"

Black stepped inside, just a few paces. "I knew you had secrets, Professor. But this?" His voice was low, tight. He nodded toward the corpse. "You keeping him as a souvenir?"

Yehohanan didn't flinch, his gaze on the body, his face a blank mask. Moore straightened, hands trembling, but her voice stayed calm.

"He was supposed to be gone," she said flatly.

Black took another step, his eyes never leaving her. "Yeah, well, he's not. And you're in deeper than you let on."

Moore crossed her arms, staring at the body as if it were just an inconvenience. "You don't understand."

"Make me understand."

Silence filled the space between them, thick with tension. Moore shook her head, her cool demeanor slipping for just a moment. "This wasn't part of the plan."

Black glanced at Yehohanan, who still hadn't spoken, his eyes glued to the body like it held the answers to a question only he knew.

"What's his story?" Black asked, nodding toward the corpse.

Moore's voice hardened. "He was a loose end."

Black took another step forward, his gaze flicking between the two of them. "Loose ends have a way of tightening around your neck."

Moore's lips curled into a thin smile, one that didn't reach her eyes. "Not if you cut them before they strangle you."

"You should've cut better," Black muttered, stepping closer, the tension in the room thick enough to choke. He looked at the dead man, then back at Moore. "Now you're gonna need help cleaning up your mess."

Yehohanan finally spoke, his voice low, almost a growl. "Are you in or out?"

Black stared him down for a long second, then let out a breath, his frustration simmering just beneath the surface. "In," he said, his tone cold and clipped. "But this time, we do it my way."

Moore looked up, her eyes catching his, calculating. "Deal."

The room felt darker, the weight of the decision pressing in on all of them. Black gave one last glance at the body, the knife gleaming in the dim light.

He wasn't sure how deep he'd have to go to dig his way out of this. But he knew one thing: whatever was coming next, it wasn't going to be clean.

TWENTY

Black shut the door behind him, the dull thud echoing in the small apartment. His gaze fixed on Professor Moore as she reached for a cigarette, lighting it with shaky hands. Smoke curled around her as she let out a sigh, her eyes narrowing at the dead man on the floor.

"That's one of Sheek's boys," she finally said, her voice cold. "He came by to rough me up. Didn't end well."

Black crossed his arms, his patience thin. "I'm starting to think I was right about walking away."

Yehohanan shifted, the discomfort plain on his face. "Maybe... maybe you were," he muttered, eyes glued to the floor.

Moore's lips twisted into a cruel smile. "Oh, don't get soft on me now, Yeho. You're in this whether you like it or not. Same as Black." She exhaled, letting the smoke drift lazily between them, her gaze hardening as she turned to Yehohanan. "Deal with it."

Yehohanan's jaw clenched, his fists balling at his sides. "And who's gonna make me?"

Her laughter was sharp, humorless. "You know, I've told my co-workers all about you. How you were coming home after all those years. How I hadn't seen you in decades, and how I hoped you'd adjust." She smiled, her eyes gleaming with something darker. "But they were worried. Told me I should be careful around you. You know how it is when men get institutionalized."

Yehohanan flinched, his face betraying the sting of her words. Moore took another drag of her cigarette, eyes never leaving his. "They were actually concerned you'd hurt me, can you believe that?"

She let the moment hang, savoring it. "I eased their worries. Sent them pictures of you. Just in case anything happens to me."

Yehohanan didn't say a word. His face said it all—hurt, betrayal, disbelief. She'd cornered him, and he knew it.

"Well, there's that," Moore said, her tone almost casual. She finally turned to Black, her smirk fading. "And you. Why are you back here?"

Black's stare was like stone. "Like it or not, we're in this together."

Moore's lips curled into a mocking smile as she flicked ash from her cigarette. "Oh, we're all in it now, huh?" She leaned back, her gaze challenging. "So, what's the next move, great detective?"

Black stepped closer, his voice low, gritty. "First, we clean up this mess. Then, we handle Sheek."

Moore's eyes glinted as she took a long drag, exhaling slowly. "Guess we'll see, won't we?"

The room was thick with tension, the kind that could break at any moment. The dead man at their feet was just the beginning, and they all knew it. This wasn't just about surviving anymore—it was about who was willing to cross the line first. And none of them were clean.

TWENTY-ONE

B lack's eyes swept the room as he thought. His gaze lingered for a moment on an old, worn-out chess set near the corner, but what caught his attention wasn't the game—it was the large, heavy-looking chest beneath it. It stood out. The chest looked sturdy, large enough to stash something—or someone. He glanced at Professor Moore, whose eyes had followed his.

"That chest," he said, nodding toward it. "Where's it go?"

Moore flicked her cigarette, a slight smile tugging at her lips. "Storage. Got a whole basement unit downstairs."

Black's eyes narrowed. He'd been in situations like this before. People always had a place, something they thought could make their problems disappear.

"Get it cleaned out. We're moving the body," he said flatly, his voice clipped and cold.

Moore didn't argue, just nodded and moved to gather some cleaning supplies. Black knelt down, inspecting the chest. He motioned to Yehohanan. "We're gonna need some muscle."

Together, they lifted the body, stuffing it awkwardly into the chest. The man's limp limbs contorted into unnatural angles, and the metallic scent of blood clung to the air, thick and suffocating. Yehohanan grunted as they forced the lid shut, locking the corpse away.

"Let's move," Black muttered.

Once they were out in the hallway, lugging the chest toward the elevator, the weight between them seemed to mirror the heavy tension in the air. Black glanced at Yehohanan, who was sweating slightly but silent, his eyes forward, face grim.

"So, this is where we are now, huh?" Black broke the silence, his tone flat but probing.

Yehohanan gave a low grunt in response, not looking at him. "Seems like it."

Black chuckled dryly. "You know, man, I didn't ask for this. And from the looks of it, neither did you."

Yehohanan finally looked at Black, his eyes dark but steady. "No, I didn't. But now we're both here."

They moved in silence for a moment longer, the weight of the chest dragging against the floor, a reminder of the mess they were in. Black spoke again, this time softer. "Why not say fuck it and run?"

Yehohanan hesitated, his jaw working like he was chewing on something bitter. He finally spoke, his voice a quiet growl. "I didn't spend 75% of my adult life behind bars to come home and spend the rest of it on the run, I'm too old for that shit and despite what Mandy was alluding to I have no desire to go back."

Black nodded, understanding his dilemma.

Yehohanan glanced at him sideways. "And you? Why didn't you walk away?"

Black laughed, but it was humorless, a dry rasp in the dark. "I don't even know this woman. Met her yesterday, and here I am, moving a body down a goddamn hallway like it's a Sunday chore. Like it or not, I'm in it if I can't get Sheek his money that he thinks I have I'm pretty much a dead man on borrowed time."

The tension between them loosened a bit, the weight of their situation binding them more than any words could. Black and Yehohanan weren't friends—not yet—but they were two men caught in the same web, with only one way out.

"Look," Black said, his voice dropping low. "This ain't over. That woman in there? She'll get what's coming to her, people like her always do."

They finally made it to the elevator, the doors creaking open. As they stepped inside, Black glanced at Yehohanan, who stared straight ahead, his expression unreadable.

"Ever been in deep like this before?" Black asked, his tone less confrontational now, more reflective.

Yehohanan sighed, a deep sound that echoed through the small space. "Not like this."

"Then let's make sure it's the last time."

The elevator lurched as it descended, the sound of gears grinding against their fate. The basement loomed ahead, the cold, dark reality of what they had to do settling between them like the weight of the chest they carried.

TWENTY-TWO

B lack wiped the sweat from his forehead after stashing the body. The weight of it wasn't just in the chest they'd moved to the basement—it clung to him, heavy on his mind. Every step he took upstairs felt like he was carrying the dead man's weight on his shoulders, not just in his arms.

By the time he reached Professor Moore's apartment, the knot of frustration in his chest was tight, pulling at the edges of his patience. When he opened the door, there she was, as if nothing had happened. She sat in the dim light of her apartment, cigarette smoke curling lazily around her, her expression as cold as ever. Her eyes flicked up when she saw him, but she didn't speak.

Black wasted no time. "Alright, Professor," he said, his tone hard and unforgiving. "Let's cut the bullshit. I need the key to that Bitcoin account."

Yehohnan's gaze remained fixed on them both, his silence unnerving. It was as if he were waiting for something to crack, for someone to push too far. Moore took a slow drag of her cigarette, the end glowing red in the dim light. She didn't flinch, didn't rush to explain herself.

When she finally spoke, her voice was calm, cool. "And I need my daughter back."

The audacity of her words twisted something deep inside Black. He stepped closer, his voice lowering to a growl. "You give me the account details, and I'll handle Sheek. But if you're keeping me in the dark, I walk. And when I walk, I won't be looking back."

She didn't move, just gave him that same cold smile, her lips barely curling around the cigarette. "You walk, Black, and we're all dead. Including your precious moral high ground."

Black leaned against the table, trying a different approach. "Listen, I don't give a damn about your games, but I care about that kid. We can't afford any more mistakes. Just give me what I need. Let me get Sheek off your back, and we'll figure out the rest."

For the first time, something in her expression softened, but only slightly. She stubbed out her cigarette, standing up. "You think I don't want this to end? You think I like playing the villain in my own story? But I don't have the code. If I did, we wouldn't be having this conversation."

Black stared at her for a long moment, searching her face for any crack in her armor, any sign she was lying. He found nothing. She was cold, calculating—yet he could see the weight of her own desperation clinging to her just as much as it was to him.

He let out a sharp breath, straightening up. "Fine. But I'm done for tonight. We'll regroup in the morning."

Without another word, he walked out, the door clicking shut behind him. He needed sleep. Time to think. But as he made his way through the empty streets, the weight of the night hung on him like a noose.

Walking away from Moore wasn't just about the case anymore—it had become personal. The way she toyed with him, giving him just enough to keep him from leaving, reminded him too much of the ghosts he couldn't shake. His mother's face hovered at the edge of his mind, the old wound of abandonment flaring up in the silence of the drive. She'd done the same—dangled hope in front of him, then vanished without a goodbye. Twice. First as a kid, and again as a man.

That's why he couldn't walk away. It wasn't just about the job. It was about refusing to be left behind again.

He drove on autopilot, his body moving through the motions while his mind circled around the same thoughts, dragging him back to the past. By the time he arrived at Deborah's place, he was already exhausted, and he needed an outlet. Something to clear the noise.

She greeted him with a warm smile, her arms wrapping around him without question. She didn't need to ask what was going on. They both knew why he was there. The release was quick, physical, but it didn't silence the storm inside him. No matter how hard he tried to lose himself in her, the weight of the night clung to him. After a couple of hours, it was clear—this wasn't going to help.

He left her place as quietly as he'd come, heading home to shower, change, and try to get his head straight before he had to pick up Stone and her daughter from the hospital.

As Black pulled into the hospital parking lot, the sterile smell of antiseptic hit him the moment he walked through the doors. It wasn't the first time he'd been in a place like this, but every time, it made his skin crawl. The lights were too bright, the air too cold, and the silence too loud. He scanned the room and spotted Saphire first, her head down, avoiding eye contact.

And next to her was someone new.

Her cousin.

Kiana from Youngstown, Ohio. Short and sexy like Stone, but with an edge that was all her own. She had long blonde extensions, a small scar near the bottom of her lip, and a plaid halter top and matching skirt that hugged her curves. Sneakers, ready for a fight. And that attitude—aggressive, like she'd been waiting to size him up and put him in his place.

"So, you're the infamous Black," Kiana said, crossing her arms, her eyes sharp as knives. "Saphire called me last night. Told me what's going on. I'm staying in town for a few weeks to help out."

Black didn't respond. He began gathering Stone's things. Kiana snorted, stepping closer, her posture daring him to say something. Saphire, standing between them, winced, her gaze glued to the floor. It was clear she knew she'd overstepped by calling Kiana, but it was too late now. Kiana was here, and she was looking for a fight.

Stone, still pale from her hospital stay, gave Black a look. That silent plea. **Be nice.**

Black sighed, rolling his shoulders to release the tension. He could feel Kiana's eyes on him, watching him like a hawk waiting to pounce, but he wasn't in the mood to give her what she wanted. Not tonight.

"Alright," he said, his voice tight. "Let's get her home."

Kiana smirked like she'd won, but Black let it slide. He just wanted to get Stone back to her place and out of this damn hospital. He helped her into the car, the ride back filled with tense silence, Kiana's sharp eyes boring into him from the backseat like she was waiting for him to slip.

Once they were at Stone's place, Black helped her inside, his mind still racing from everything that had happened. Stone shot him a grateful glance as they settled her in, but the tension in the air was thick—unspoken words hanging between them like a wall.

Kiana leaned against the doorframe, arms crossed, her gaze fixed on Black, sharp and unyielding. "You gonna be around this time, Black? Or is this another one of your disappearing acts?"

Black chuckled, a low, dangerous sound that barely masked his irritation. His patience was stretched thin, and Kiana was pressing all the wrong buttons. "Stay in your lane, Kiana, and we won't have any problems."

She cocked an eyebrow, unfazed. "My lane? And what if I decide to step out of it?"

Before Black could respond, Stone's voice cut through the tension like a blade. "Enough." Her tone was cold, sharp, laced with authority that demanded attention. She turned to Kiana, her expression hard. "You're here to help me, not to pick fights. You've been running your mouth since you walked in the door, and I'm tired of it."

Kiana opened her mouth to fire back, but Stone didn't give her the chance.

"Don't talk to him like that," Stone continued, her voice firm. "The only reason he's tolerating your attitude is because of me. So back off before you push things too far. We've got enough shit to deal with without adding your ego to the pile."

Kiana stared at her for a beat, the tension in the room thick enough to choke on. But Stone's words hung heavy, a warning neither of them could ignore. Kiana's jaw tightened, but she stayed quiet, her arms uncrossing as she took a small step back, clearly weighing her next move.

Black met Kiana's gaze one last time, then turned his attention to Stone. His expression softened, just a touch, as if to say, *Thanks.* But the silence between them said more than words ever could.

It was a fragile peace, but for now, it was enough to keep the storm at bay.

TWENTY-THREE

Anthony Drake stood on the balcony of his downtown Chicago apartment, staring out at the sprawling skyline that glittered beneath him. The city looked different from up here, almost peaceful. But Drake knew better. He'd been down there in the dirt, clawing his way through the streets, surviving prisons, failed businesses, and betrayals. Now, as the cool night air brushed against his face, he felt something he hadn't felt in a long time: power.

It had all started six months ago. He'd just gotten out of FCI Memphis, another stint in the system that felt like a death sentence for most. But for Drake, it was just another bump in the road. He'd always fancied himself a businessman—failure was just a learning experience. So what if he'd lost money, been stabbed in the back, and wound up in prison? To him, it all prepared him for this exact moment. He'd finally gotten his break.

His first day out, no money, no job, no place to stay. He'd been feeling that familiar anxiety rising in his chest—the pressure to figure out his next move before he ended up back in the same cycle. But then Malik Johnson appeared out of nowhere. A man of means, of influence, and for reasons Drake didn't understand at the time, Malik had taken him under his wing.

Drake still remembered that first meeting like it was yesterday. He'd been sitting on a bench, trying to figure out how to hustle up some cash, when Malik strolled by, like an angel in a tailored suit. There had been something different about him, a calm, measured energy. Malik didn't carry the aggression of the streets, didn't flaunt his wealth like so many others who had escaped the grind. No, Malik was something else—a man who moved in silence but with power. A man who helped without expectation.

"You're gonna need a second chance," Malik had said that day. "I know some people in Chicago—important people. When the time comes, you'll be in a position to help me out, and when I ask, you'll say yes. No questions."

Drake had taken Malik's number that day, not expecting anything from it. He figured Malik was like most people who talked big but never followed through. But two days later, Malik showed up at the rundown rooming house Drake had crashed in, holding the keys to a brand-new truck, travel money, and the lease to an apartment in the heart of Chicago.

Drake had yet to meet these mysterious "people" Malik spoke of, but it didn't matter. Malik had delivered, and Drake was smart enough to see the opportunity. No one gives you a free ride for nothing, and whatever Malik wanted, Drake would do it. That kind of generosity came with strings, but as long as Drake kept climbing, he didn't care. He was no stranger to making deals with devils. And if this was a coup against Sheek, well, all the better. Sheek had power, sure, but even a king could fall if you hit him in the right spot.

Drake's eyes scanned the horizon, taking in the twinkling lights of the city. He could almost feel the pieces coming together—Black Love,

Amanda Moore, and Sheek, all pawns in a game they didn't know they were playing. And him? He was the puppet master pulling the strings.

The briefcase Malik had given him last night was the next step. It hadn't been cash, though. It had been something much more dangerous: fentanyl. A sample, enough to distribute to the crews operating in and around Chicago, to bring them on board. The drug trade wasn't new to Drake—he'd been in and out of it for years—but this was different. This was the start of something big. Malik was planning to take over Chicago's underground, and Drake was going to be right there with him when the dust settled.

But there was one major obstacle: Sheek.

Sheek had built his empire on fear, loyalty, and ruthlessness. He ruled with an iron fist, and there was one unbreakable rule in his kingdom—no drugs. Selling narcotics in Sheek's territory was a death sentence, no questions asked. It didn't matter if you were a low-level street soldier or a trusted lieutenant. Violate that rule, and Sheek would make you disappear.

Drake knew he was treading on thin ice. If Sheek even got a whiff of what was happening, it wouldn't just be his empire that crumbled—Drake's life would be over. But Malik had promised protection, and so far, he hadn't let Drake down. The trick was getting enough of Sheek's crews on board without tipping Sheek off. If Drake played this right, Sheek wouldn't know what hit him until it was too late.

Leaning against the balcony railing, Drake felt a surge of adrenaline. It was all coming together. Black and Amanda were tangled up in their own messes, and soon enough, their paths would collide with Sheek's in a way that would destroy all of them. And Drake? He'd be left standing, watching the city burn as he stepped over the ashes.

The phone in his pocket buzzed, pulling him out of his thoughts. He checked the screen—it was Malik.

"You make the drop?" Malik's voice was smooth, controlled, just like the man himself.

"Yeah," Drake replied. "Everything's in motion."

There was a pause, then Malik spoke again, his voice a little harder this time. "Good. Just remember—no mistakes. Sheek finds out, and you're dead before I can help you."

Drake smirked, feeling the familiar rush of danger course through him. "I've got it under control."

"You better," Malik said, his tone final. "Because if you slip, I can't save you from what's coming."

The line went dead, and Drake pocketed his phone, staring back out at the city. Malik was right—there was no room for mistakes. Sheek wasn't the kind of man you could double-cross and walk away from. But Drake had spent his whole life betting on himself, and this was just another high-stakes gamble.

As he stood there, the wind picking up around him, Drake allowed himself a moment of satisfaction. He'd been at the bottom, forgotten and written off. But now? Now, he was a player in a game that could change everything.

The thought made him smile. Let Black and Amanda play their roles. Let Sheek run his empire like he was untouchable. By the time they realized what was happening, it would be too late.

Drake lifted his glass, toasting the Chicago skyline.

"To the king," he muttered, his smile widening.

Because soon, Sheek's throne would be his.

TWENTY-FOUR

P rofessor Moore woke with a start, her body heavy with the weight of another sleepless night. The clock on the nightstand blinked 4 a.m. in red, glaring like an accusation. She groaned and pushed herself out of bed, her feet dragging across the cold hardwood floor. The apartment was eerily quiet, the type of silence that clung to you in the early hours before dawn.

She shuffled toward the kitchen, needing coffee, something to jolt her out of the fog that clouded her thoughts. As she crossed through the living room and reached for the light switch, her hand froze mid-air.

Yehohnan was sitting there, fully dressed, motionless, staring at the black screen of the television like it was playing something only he could see. His broad shoulders were hunched, his back straight, as if he were waiting for a cue, the flicker of a forgotten program that never started. Moore's breath caught in her throat. She raised an eyebrow but didn't say a word. A man like Yehohnan didn't need explanations, and she wasn't about to ask him what the hell he was doing. There were some things you just let be.

She flipped on the light, illuminating the room in a harsh yellow glow. The shadows softened, but the tension in the air thickened. She moved to the kitchen, and without looking back, called over her shoulder, "Coffee?"

Yehohnan didn't turn. "Tell me how you got into this mess in the first place," he said, his voice flat, no curiosity behind it—just an expectation that she would answer.

Moore's hands shook as she reached for the coffee grounds. She steadied herself, poured them into the filter, and set the machine to brew. She leaned against the counter, her eyes tracing the outline of his back from across the room.

"I got tired of scraping by," she started. "Saw an opportunity to get ahead and took it. Sheek's people came to me—wanted help hiding his money. His distilleries, under-the-table businesses, the kind of stuff that keeps people like me in business." She paused, glancing toward him, but he didn't move. "So I took a little off the top."

Yehohnan's head tilted, ever so slightly. "Until?"

Moore let out a sharp breath, pushing herself away from the counter. "Until it wasn't just a little off the top anymore. I got greedy. He must've noticed. So I put together an insurance plan in case things went sideways."

The machine beeped, signaling the coffee was ready. She poured two cups, the steam curling into the air between them. Yehohnan finally turned his head, just enough to glance at her from the corner of his eye.

"How's that insurance plan been working out for you?" he asked, his voice dripping with cold sarcasm.

She didn't answer. Instead, she changed the subject. "You sleep alright?"

He didn't respond, didn't so much as twitch. His eyes slid back to the darkened window, the city outside barely waking up beneath the pale glow of streetlights.

Moore sighed, walking over to him, the mugs clutched tightly in her hands. She placed one on the table beside him. He didn't acknowledge it. She sat in the chair across from him, holding her own cup, her fingers warming around the ceramic.

"Why don't you take your chances and walk away?" she asked, the question soft but cutting through the silence like a knife.

His back still to her, Yehohnan's voice was low, rough. "Why did you feel you needed to blackmail me instead of asking for help?"

Moore froze, the coffee inches from her lips. His words hit harder than she expected. She set the cup down, carefully, deliberately.

"I guess I figured you'd given so much already," she said after a long pause, her eyes focused on his silhouette. "Didn't feel like I had the right to ask for more. So I did what I thought I had to do. People take what they want. Whether it's inside or out—doesn't matter. Con or civilian. When someone wants something, why ask when you can just take it?"

Yehohnan was quiet, the kind of quiet that made her stomach twist. She wanted him to say something, anything, to break the tension, but the silence stretched. Finally, he moved, standing up from the couch and walking to the window. He stared out at the empty streets, the world still caught between night and day, caught in that space where shadows could hide almost anything.

"You still didn't answer my question," he said, his voice barely above a whisper. "Threat or no threat, you could've walked away."

Moore leaned back in her chair, watching him carefully, trying to gauge his mood. Yehohnan was a fortress, but she'd seen enough cracks to know something was burning inside. He turned then, finally facing her. His eyes were dark, heavy with something she couldn't quite name.

"Yeah," he continued, his gaze hard. "But I didn't give my life to save your daughter just to turn around and let her die if I could help her."

She blinked, surprised by the intensity of his words. "Even at the risk of losing your own life?" Her voice wavered just a little, caught off guard by the weight of his conviction.

His lips twitched into a cold smile, one that didn't reach his eyes. "Almost sounds Christianly, don't it?"

The words hung between them, sharp and biting, like the air in the room had turned colder. Moore took a slow sip from her coffee, her mind racing, searching for something to say that could cut through the quiet, the tension.

But she didn't have an answer. Not for him. Not for herself.

Outside, the first light of dawn began to creep across the sky, turning the dark blue into a cold, steel-gray. And for the first time in a long time, Moore wondered if maybe—just maybe—she'd already lost, and she was the last one to realize it.

TWENTY-FIVE

B lack stepped through the front door of Pops' house, his mind still heavy from the night's chaos. As he entered, the familiar scent of home wrapped around him, but something was different. His eyes caught small details that weren't there the last time he visited—a pair of small-sized women's running shoes sat neatly by the front door, just next to Pops' well-worn boots. On the sofa, a cardigan and some women's clothing were draped over the backrest, carelessly left as if the owner planned to return at any moment.

His brow furrowed slightly as he walked through the living room, but he didn't say anything. He wasn't here to pry into Pops' personal life, though the evidence seemed hard to miss now. He moved toward the kitchen, where the final clue confirmed what he already knew—a pair of women's reading glasses sat on the counter. He processed the signs of the quiet domesticity that had crept into Pops' life. He didn't mention any of it to Pops. It wasn't his business.

Sparkle, Pops' white Pitbull, bounded up to him, full of excitement. Black gave her a quick pat, his mind still swirling with thoughts. Walking into the kitchen, the weight of the night's events lingered in his chest, tangled up with everything he couldn't say out loud—about Sheek, about Moore, and especially about Stone.

Pops was sitting at the table, his focus on the television as the Chicago Cubs played in the background. A worn copy of *Aid State: Elite Panic, Disaster Capitalism, and The Battle to Control Haiti* by Jake Johnston sat next to a Hoagy Cheesesteak and fries drenched in mild sauce. Black leaned down, kissing the top of his father's head before pulling out a chair beside him.

"What's going on, boy? You ain't been by in a while," Pops said, his eyes never leaving the screen.

"Been busy, Pops. You been good?"

"Yeah, been doin' more walking lately. Me and the girl." Pops nodded toward Sparkle, who lifted her head at the sound of her name, her eyes full of attention.

Black chuckled, but when Pops caught the sound, he looked over with a raised brow. "What's funny?"

"Sparkle ain't the only girl you been walking with," Black teased, a grin playing at the edges of his mouth.

"Boy, hush," Pops said, shaking his head. "I heard about you and Ms. Jackson. Moved in across the street, huh?"

"You bein' silly."

"If you say so."

"I do."

Pops shook his head, turning his attention back to the game for a moment before the familiar look of concern crossed his face. "Speakin' of women," he started, turning his gaze back to Black. "You hop around so much, who is it now?"

Black laughed, leaning back in his chair. "It ain't like that, Pops."

"What's it like, then?"

"Weighing my options."

Pops grunted, leaning forward as if the words irritated him. "Options is another way of sayin' fear of committing."

Black shrugged, unfazed. "I am committing, Pops. I'm committing to myself."

"And what about the Stone girl? What about her?"

Black shifted in his seat, not quite ready to dive into that subject. "What about her?"

"Why not her? I mean, other than all them kids. She got, what, four?"

"Yeah. I don't know, Pops. It's a work in progress."

Pops let out a low laugh, shaking his head. "Aren't they all? And what about the white girl? What's her name? Deborah?"

"Yeah," Black muttered, the name tasting like it didn't belong in this conversation.

"She's a doctor, ain't she?" Pops pushed, like he was ticking off boxes in his mind. "What's wrong with her?"

"Too clingy."

Pops laughed, the kind of deep, belly laugh that echoed in the small kitchen. "Boy, you crack me up. I know what it is."

"Oh, you do?" Black leaned forward, intrigued by the confidence in Pops' voice. "What is it, then?"

"You still got your mind on Trigger."

Black's smile faltered, just for a second, but Pops caught it. He always did. Black shook his head, trying to brush it off. "Nah, Pops. If something was gonna happen between me and Trigger, it would've by now."

Pops gave him a knowing look, one that said more than words ever could. "Umm hmm," he muttered, turning back to the Cubs game.

That was the thing—Trigger was like a shadow, always lingering at the edge of his life. No matter how much he tried to move forward, she was there, haunting him. It was the same with Stone. He couldn't commit to her either, not fully. Because, deep down, he wasn't just afraid of commitment. He was afraid of losing again. Afraid that committing meant giving someone the power to leave him behind. Again.

Just like his mother.

That was the parallel that stung the most. Just like Pops had found some semblance of peace, some stability in the quiet presence of another woman, Black was constantly chasing chaos. And he didn't know how to stop.

The thought gnawed at him as he sat there, the Cubs game buzzing in the background. It was the same story over and over—whether it was Trigger, Stone, or even Deborah, they were all just reminders of what he couldn't have. And maybe, deep down, what he didn't believe he deserved.

Pops didn't need to say more. His silence, his steadiness, spoke volumes. Black looked at him and realized that while Pops had found his peace, Black was still caught in the storm. The women in his life—Stone, Deborah, even Trigger—they were all part of that storm. And until he figured out how to calm it, he'd keep drifting, searching for something he wasn't even sure existed.

The conversation died out after that, but the weight of it lingered. Black stood, giving Sparkle another pat as he headed for the door. But before he left, he glanced back at Pops, who was still watching the game as if nothing had changed.

But something had. And Black knew it.

He walked out, the pressures of the case and a longing for his own version of domestic life pressing in on him like a second skin, that same nagging thought in his head—commitment. It was a word that tasted foreign in his mouth. Something Pops seemed to understand, even if Black didn't.

And yet, the evidence was there, scattered throughout the house—running shoes, glasses, and a woman's presence that spoke of something more. Something solid. Maybe that was what Black was missing all along.

But today, he wasn't ready to face it.

He stepped out into the world, eyes wide open into the heart of the storm.

TWENTY-SIX

J oanne sat at her desk, tapping absentmindedly at the keyboard, though her mind was elsewhere. Across the room, Johnny sat slouched in a chair, flipping through his phone, looking as bored as any teenager would. The office was quiet, just the occasional click of a keyboard or the hum of the printer breaking the silence. Small talk had come easy earlier—usual banter about school and nonsense—but now, Joanne's thoughts were firmly fixed on something more serious.

She glanced over at Johnny, who was still preoccupied with his phone, and her mind wandered back to the day she'd met that kid. The boy from Johnny's school. His nervous grin and awkward attempts at flirting had been almost endearing.

It hadn't taken much. A few likes on his stories, some comments on his posts. Before long, he was messaging her, excited to meet up. The conversation that followed over coffee had been revealing—and disturbing. The boy had been through hell, but Johnny's name had come up, and that had sparked a different kind of emotion in her.

She looked down at her own phone, replaying the scene in her mind: the timid kid sitting across from her, looking grateful for the first friendly face he'd seen in a while, spilling his story. He had a bruise on his face, the kind you couldn't just brush off as an accident. And Johnny was at the center of it all—his name mentioned like some kind of savior.

Johnny had stepped in, stopped the bullying, and made sure the kid was safe. It was something Black would want to know about, but Johnny had kept it quiet. Too quiet.

"So," she said, breaking the silence in the room. Johnny glanced up, not expecting the sudden shift in her tone. "That kid you helped out... the one with the bruise? What's his story?"

Johnny froze for a second, his face going blank. "What kid?"

Joanne leaned back in her chair, crossing her arms. "Don't play dumb with me, Johnny. I met him. The one from your school. He told me everything."

Johnny sat up straighter, his jaw tensing. "How do you know about that?"

She shrugged, playing it cool. "I have my ways."

He glared at her, but she could see the gears turning in his head. He didn't like that she knew. "It's not a big deal."

"Not a big deal?" Joanne raised an eyebrow. "You stepped in and fought off a group of guys. You didn't think Black would want to hear about that?"

Johnny shook his head, his expression hardening. "Don't make a big deal out of it, Joanne."

She studied him for a moment. There was something different about Johnny right now—something more serious, more resolved than she had seen before. She wasn't used to seeing him like this, so determined to keep quiet about something.

"Why are you being stupid about this?" she pressed, her tone softening slightly. "You did the right thing, Johnny. Black would understand that. Why not just tell him?"

Johnny's eyes narrowed. "Because I broke the rules. I knew the rules, and I broke them. It doesn't matter if I think I was right. Rules are rules."

Joanne leaned forward, her voice dropping to a near whisper. "You think Black wouldn't understand why you did it? He's always been about standing up for what's right."

Johnny shook his head again, more firmly this time. "It's not about whether or not he'd understand. It's about me taking responsibility. I broke the rules, and I'll take whatever punishment comes with that."

Joanne paused, watching him carefully. There was a new kind of determination in his eyes, something she hadn't seen before. The boy who usually acted like nothing could touch him was gone, replaced by someone willing to face consequences, no matter how tough they were. It was an odd sense of honor, but it struck her hard. She felt a small flicker of pride swell in her chest, though she'd never let him know that.

"Well," she said, shaking her head. "You're crazy." Johnny didn't flinch, just stared her down with that same serious expression. Joanne sighed, leaning back in her chair. "But I'll keep it to myself. You've got guts, I'll give you that."

Johnny's posture relaxed slightly, though the tension still lingered in the room. Joanne watched him for a moment, marveling at the maturity she hadn't expected. He wasn't as goofy or reckless as she'd always assumed. This was a different side of Johnny—one that took her by surprise.

She turned back to her screen, her fingers tapping lightly against the keys, but her mind was still on Johnny and his stubborn sense of responsibility. He had stepped up when it counted, and while he might not want Black to know, Joanne knew she'd be keeping a closer eye on him from now on. There was more to Johnny than met the eye.

TWENTY-SEVEN

T he sound of tape ripping filled the room as Stone and Kiana sat on the floor surrounded by cardboard boxes from Amazon, their contents spilling out in piles—baby clothes, wipes, a car seat, baby towels, and bottles all ready for the new arrival. Stone was folding tiny onesies for both a boy and a girl, her hands moving methodically while Kiana sat cross-legged, holding up a pair of baby socks with a smirk.

"Another baby, huh?" Kiana teased, eyeing the sea of pastel fabrics. "Your oldest is off to college, and your youngest is ten. Girl, you out here starting over like a damn rookie."

Stone shrugged, her expression calm as she folded another onesie. "It is what it is," she said, her tone dismissive but not without a hint of weariness.

Kiana leaned back, tossing the socks into the pile with a laugh. "You say that like it's no big deal. So, how did you and Black meet anyway? Was it all fireworks and drama from the jump?"

Stone shook her head, a small smile playing on her lips. "Nah, he came into my job with his girl."

Kiana's eyes widened with mock shock. "Ooh girl, you a home-wrecker?" She leaned in closer, waggling her eyebrows.

They both burst out laughing, the sound filling the small living room.

Stone nudged her playfully. "No, it was nothing like that."

Kiana rolled her eyes, her grin still in place. "If you say so."

"Well, I do," Stone replied, her tone firm but playful.

Kiana wasn't letting it go, though. She leaned in again, her voice dropping to a conspiratorial whisper. "You and that other chick ever crossed paths?"

Stone shook her head. "Nope. Never met her."

"Well," Kiana said, folding her arms across her chest, "let's hope it stays that way. Bitch gets froggy, she'll end up like Rashonda back home."

Stone groaned, shaking her head with a laugh. "Oh Lord, don't put my name on that foolishness. I'm not claiming no parts of that."

"Girl, you act like I put hands on her," Kiana said, feigning innocence.

"Might as well have," Stone shot back. "You could've called your wolves off."

Kiana's eyes twinkled with mischief. "Hmm, she got pregnant 'cause I got pregnant. Latrell ain't care nothin' about either of us, and your little crew of hoodlums jumped that girl."

Stone let out a low sigh, her head shaking in disbelief. "Six months pregnant and y'all tried to stomp that baby out of her. Y'all lucky she didn't lose that baby. All of y'all would've gone down behind that mess. I do not miss Youngstown."

Kiana snorted. "Not even a little bit?"

"Nope. Life is good here."

Kiana raised an eyebrow, her voice teasing. "That's not what Saphire says."

Stone's face tightened, her hands pausing mid-fold. "Don't worry about what she's talking about. I'll have words with her later."

"Girl, don't give my little cousin a hard time," Kiana said, waving her off. "She's just worried about you. Wants you to be happy."

Stone pursed her lips, her eyes narrowing slightly. "That girl knows better than to be spreading my business."

Kiana smiled, shaking her head. "Stop it. So, you're not happy I'm here?"

Stone glanced at her, the smallest hint of a grin pulling at the corners of her mouth. "Yeah."

"Then shut your ass up complaining, then."

Stone burst out laughing. "Girl, forget you."

They fell into a comfortable silence for a moment, the sounds of crinkling paper and boxes being opened filling the room. Kiana reached for another package, her voice suddenly excited. "You know who I seen the other day?"

Stone didn't even look up, rolling her eyes. "Keep it to yourself."

Kiana's grin was devilish. "He was lookin' good. And asking about you."

Stone finally glanced up, her voice flat. "He knows how to get in touch with me."

Kiana sat back, a little smug. "He said he'd take you back. Said leaving you and the kids was the biggest mistake of his life. When's the last time you saw him?"

Stone shrugged, her fingers still working through the baby clothes. Truth was she'd just seen him about two weeks ago, he'd been staying there. She was about 90% sure the baby she was carrying was probably his, she willed in her mind and soul that it was Black's, and she was going with that. "Try not to think about it."

Kiana watched her for a moment, her gaze softening. "What about you and Black?" she asked gently.

Stone looked up, her eyes meeting Kiana's. "What about him?"

"What are y'all gonna do?"

Stone sighed, her shoulders lifting slightly before falling again. "I don't know. Play it by ear."

Kiana didn't push. She could see the exhaustion behind Stone's eyes, the weight of everything she was carrying. Instead, she reached over and gave her a light nudge. "Just want you to know," Kiana said, her voice soft but steady, "Youngstown is always home. If you gotta come back, we'll work it out together. As a family."

Stone smiled, a real smile this time, one that reached her eyes. "Yeah, I know."

"Then shut up and quit complainin'," Kiana said with a smirk.

Stone laughed, shaking her head. "Girl, forget you."

Twenty-Eight

Sheek Green stirred in his hotel penthouse suite, the kind of room that dripped with opulence. Marble floors, gold accents, furniture that cost more than most people's yearly salaries. But the luxury was lost on him this morning. It wasn't the decor or the extravagant spread of breakfast in the next room that weighed on his mind. It was something heavier, something lurking just beyond the silk sheets.

The soft *whoosh* of the curtains being drawn filled the room, and a flood of sunlight invaded his sanctuary. Sheek scrunched his face, burying it beneath a pillow to shield himself from the light.

"Up and at 'em, Mr. Green," came the smooth, commanding voice of his assistant—his lover too, when it suited them both. She moved around the room with purpose, scooping up discarded clothing, her heels clicking against the floor. Always efficient, always poised. Her black business pantsuit fit her like a second skin, sharp and professional, but there was nothing purely business about her.

He groaned into the pillow but didn't move.

"Your fitness trainer will be here any minute. Busy day, let's go," she continued, her voice cutting through the room like the blade of a knife.

He sighed, the sound deep, gruff, reluctant, as he slowly sat up, letting the blanket fall from his chest. He was Sheek Green, and nothing happened without his say-so. But today, even his usual stubbornness was bending under the weight of everything on his mind.

Margot, his Filipino girlfriend, slipped into the room from the adjoining bathroom, her skin gleaming in the morning light, her body clad only in lace panties and a bra that barely covered her. She was a vision—curves and confidence. She leaned over the bed, giving Sheek a kiss, then moved fluidly to the assistant, pulling her in for a deep, sensual kiss that lingered far longer than necessary. The assistant responded, her posture melting for a brief moment, before straightening up as if nothing had happened.

"Long day for me too," Margot said, her voice soft but laced with ambition. "Got fabrics coming in from Milan that I want to test for my designs."

She drifted over to the dining area, where an impressive spread of fruits, pastries, and eggs awaited. She wasn't just decorative, she had her own empire to build. And like Sheek, she was hungry for more.

But Sheek wasn't listening, not really. He got out of bed, moving around the room in his usual fashion, naked and unapologetic. His muscles flexed as he stretched, his skin catching the morning light. To anyone watching, it would've looked like the beginning of a perfect day. But Sheek's mind wasn't on breakfast or fabrics or even the beautiful women sharing his space.

Margot poured him a cup of coffee, and he took it without a word, pacing slowly toward the window. He sipped it, the bitterness of the coffee sharp on his tongue, as his eyes swept over the city below. The skyline stretched out in front of him, an empire in its own right, but all he could think about was the empire he built and how close it had come to slipping through his fingers.

He needed his money.

It wasn't the money itself, he had enough of that to last lifetimes. It was the principle. The fact that someone—anyone—had the nerve to take from him. Let one thing slide, and soon everyone would think they could steal a piece of Sheek Green.

His grip tightened around the coffee cup, his jaw clenching as his thoughts darkened. His team wasn't getting it done. They were moving slow, too cautious, too comfortable in the life he provided them. He'd given them everything—power, prestige, safety—and now they were failing him when he needed them the most.

If you wanted something done right, you had to do it yourself. He'd been hands-off for too long, trusting others to handle business. That was going to change. Sheek wasn't the type to let things simmer. He didn't wait for the perfect moment, he created it. And he was about to remind everyone just who they were dealing with.

The assistant was still moving around the room, her voice occasionally floating through the air, reminding him of his schedule, the meetings, the appointments, the deals. But her words were background noise. She didn't understand what was at stake here. Margot, for all her ambition, didn't get it either. They both operated in worlds where failure was an inconvenience. In Sheek's world, failure got you killed.

He stared down at the street below, watching the ants scurry to and fro, going about their lives without a clue that men like him controlled their fate. He took another sip of coffee, the warmth settling into his chest, but his heart remained cold.

Sheek had built an empire from nothing. No connections. No handouts. Just pure, relentless ambition and the willingness to do whatever it took to stay on top. Now someone was testing him, pushing the boundaries of what they thought they could take. That was a mistake.

He heard the women behind him, laughing softly, moving about the suite like everything was fine. But Sheek was already planning, already thinking about who he needed to talk to, who needed to be put back in line.

His empire wasn't crumbling—not yet—but if he didn't make a move, it would. And if there was one thing Sheek Green didn't do, it was lose.

He downed the rest of his coffee in one gulp, setting the cup down on the window ledge with a soft thud. His assistant stopped mid-sentence, sensing the shift in the air, her eyes flicking to him cautiously.

"Mr. Green?" she asked, her voice quieter now, more careful.

He didn't answer right away, his gaze still fixed on the city below. Finally, he turned to face her, his expression hard, his eyes cold. "Cancel everything for today. I've got business to handle."

Margot, mid-bite of her croissant, raised an eyebrow but didn't say a word. The assistant nodded, moving quickly to grab her phone, already adjusting his schedule.

Sheek moved back toward the bedroom, his steps slow but deliberate. It was time to get his hands dirty again. Time to remind people who ran this city.

And God help anyone who stood in his way.

TWENTY-NINE

Professor Moore and Yehohanan sat in silence after the last bites of breakfast, the weight of the conversation pressing down on them both. The kitchen light was dim, casting long shadows over the room, leaving much unsaid between them. But they'd come to an agreement—he would help her, but for a price. There was always a price.

"Everything comes with a cost," Yehohanan had murmured, leaning back in his chair, his eyes narrowing as he stared at the remnants of his meal. "If I'm gonna risk my neck to help you get your daughter back and keep Sheek's money, I need my cut. That's the deal."

Moore had nodded, her fingers tracing the edge of her coffee cup, knowing there wasn't any other option. She wasn't naive—this was a long shot, a gamble with stakes so high that one wrong move meant certain death. But it was better than doing nothing, and Yehohanan seemed willing to play the hand.

"What's your plan then?" she had asked, her voice steady, but her eyes betraying the flicker of fear beneath the surface.

He shrugged, eyes dark. "No plan yet. But we've got twenty-four hours. We'll figure something out."

They had sat in silence for a few more minutes before Yehohanan suggested they take a walk. Said it helped him think. Moore didn't want to go—her mind was cluttered enough without stepping into the light of day—but she agreed, knowing they didn't have time to waste.

When they reached the street, the chill of early morning air hit them, sharp and biting. The sun hadn't fully risen yet, and the streets were quiet, the city still stirring from its slumber. As they stepped outside, a figure caught her eye—Chioma Musa Ibrahim, the man she had seen the other day, was standing in front of his building.

The two locked eyes, and for a moment, it felt like the world had frozen in place. Chioma was tall, nearly as tall as Yehohanan, with a body built like it had been sculpted from stone. Tattoos ran down the sides of his arms, intricate patterns that disappeared beneath his sleeves. His shirt was unbuttoned, revealing a muscular chest with a crucifix tattooed over his heart, a large beaded cross hanging from his neck. His gaze was steady, unwavering, like he was measuring her up, calculating something she didn't want to know.

Yehohanan didn't miss the exchange, his eyes flicking between them as he took in the tension. He said nothing, but his silence was enough to let her know he noticed.

They walked without speaking for a few minutes, their footsteps echoing off the sidewalk. The sounds of the city were beginning to creep in—traffic starting to hum, distant voices, the occasional barking dog—but it felt muted, as though the world hadn't quite woken up yet.

"You wanna tell me about that?" Yehohanan asked, his voice casual, but there was an edge to it.

Moore shook her head. "Not important."

He didn't push it, but she could tell he was filing it away, another piece of the puzzle he was trying to solve.

For the next hour, they tossed ideas back and forth, trying to piece together a plan that didn't exist. Every scenario felt like a dead end. Every option felt like it led them back to the same place—Sheek Green's world, a world that swallowed people whole and spat them out in pieces.

Yehohanan was the first to break the silence, his voice low and thoughtful. "Why are you doing this in the first place?"

Moore stopped walking, her breath hanging in the air for a moment before she spoke. "Because I want my piece of the American dream."

He raised an eyebrow, waiting for her to continue.

"Sheek Green takes what he wants," she said, her voice steady, but there was a heat behind it, an anger that had been simmering for a long time. "Men like him don't care about people like me. We grind, we hustle, we try to make a life, and he just takes, without a second thought. It's not right."

Yehohanan watched her, his eyes narrowing slightly. "So you figured you'd take his instead."

"Why not?" she shot back, her voice sharper now. "He doesn't deserve it. He's built his empire on the backs of people like me—people who work, people who follow the rules. Why should I sit back and watch him live a life of luxury while I scrape by? I deserve more than that."

Her words hung in the air, heavy with the weight of her resentment. Yehohanan understood that anger. He'd felt it himself more times than he cared to admit. The system wasn't made for people like them. It was rigged from the start.

"And you're not alone in this, are you?" he asked, his voice soft, but there was a keen edge to it.

Moore hesitated, just for a moment, before answering. "No. I've got help. Someone with resources. When the time's right, they'll step in."

Yehohanan tilted his head slightly, considering her words. "And you trust this person?"

She met his gaze, her eyes hard. "I trust that they want the same thing I do. A shot at something better."

He nodded slowly, but inside, he was already calculating. Whoever this person was, they were a wild card. And wild cards had a way of complicating things. But he wasn't about to walk away. Not when there was a chance, however slim, that they could pull this off.

Yehohanan glanced around at the quiet streets, the sun now rising higher in the sky, casting long shadows across the pavement. "We've got twenty-four hours," he said, his voice steady. "We're gonna need more than luck."

Moore looked at him, her jaw set. "Then we better get to work."

As they walked on, Yehohanan's mind wandered back to the brief moments when his life hadn't felt like it was teetering on the edge of collapse. Puerto Rico... he could see it now, the waves, the sun, the calm. If they pulled this off, if they got the money, he could disappear. Leave Chicago behind. No more hustling, no more scraping by. Just freedom.

But first, they had to survive the next twenty-four hours.

And in Chicago, that was easier said than done.

THIRTY

After the long walk with Yehohanan, Professor Moore sat in her dimly lit living room, her mind still spinning from their conversation. Her fingers drummed anxiously on the table as she waited for Black to call. The house felt too quiet, too still, and every passing second only fed the growing knot of dread tightening in her chest. The weight of the choices she had made—the lies, the risk, the money—it all hung over her like a dark cloud.

The sudden buzz of her phone startled her, and she grabbed it without hesitation. Her heart skipped when she saw her daughter's name flashing across the screen. Relief washed over her, and she answered on the first ring.

"Baby, where are you?" Her voice was trembling, the fear and hope mixing in her words.

But the response on the other end wasn't her daughter's. It was a man's voice, calm and clipped, with a thick Hispanic accent.

"Ma'am, this is Detective Sanchez with the Davenport Police Department. Am I speaking with Mrs. Moore?"

Professor Moore's heart stuttered in her chest, her breath catching in her throat. For a long moment, she couldn't speak. The words hung there, suspended, and the world seemed to slow around her.

The detective spoke again, his tone softening. "Mrs. Moore?"

She blinked, snapping out of her horrific thoughts. "Yes, this is Mrs. Moore."

There was a pause, just long enough to feel like the air had been sucked out of the room.

"I'm sorry to inform you, ma'am, that a body was found here in Davenport, Iowa, and we believe the deceased female may be your daughter. We would like for you to come and identify the body."

The phone slipped from her hand, clattering to the floor. She didn't respond, didn't speak—her mind couldn't process what she had just heard. The sound of her own breathing seemed distant, like she was underwater, drowning in disbelief. A second later, a scream tore from her throat, raw and unrelenting, a sound of pure agony that echoed through the small apartment.

Yehohanan rushed into the living room, his eyes scanning the scene. He saw her on her knees, her body shaking with sobs, the phone lying forgotten on the floor. The scream was one he had heard before. He had seen that same look on the faces of men in prison—men who had lost everything, unable to reach out to those they loved.

He stood there, a silent witness to her grief. There was nothing he could do, nothing he could say to make this better. So he gave her space, letting her mourn, her wails filling the empty room like a tragic hymn.

Minutes passed, though to Moore, they felt like hours. She knelt there, her face buried in her hands, her mind racing through memories of her daughter—the laughter, the arguments, the hugs, and the quiet moments of just being together. And now, the thought of her being gone was unbearable.

Yehohanan shifted slightly, stepping closer but keeping his distance. He knew this pain too well. It was the kind that gnawed at your soul, leaving scars that never truly healed. In moments like this, words were useless.

Finally, the sobs began to subside, her body trembling as she tried to pull herself together. She couldn't breathe, couldn't think. Her daughter—the thought of her lying on a cold slab in some morgue was too much to bear.

Yehohanan's voice was low and steady when he finally spoke. "You don't have to go through this alone, you know. Whatever you need, I'm here."

Moore didn't respond right away, her body still shaking. After a long pause, she looked up at him, her eyes red and puffy, but filled with a grim determination.

"I need to go to Davenport," she whispered, her voice hoarse.

He nodded. "We'll figure it out."

As the silence settled back into the room, Moore wiped her face with trembling hands, forcing herself to stand. She couldn't afford to fall apart now—not when there was still a chance her daughter was alive. And if she wasn't, she'd find out who did this.

One way or another, they would pay.

THIRTY-ONE

B lack gripped the steering wheel tighter as he headed toward the south side of Chicago. His mind swirled with everything Pops had said. One thing had become clear—he was a pawn in a game where he didn't even know the rules. And Black? He wasn't anybody's pawn.

Lion Mohamed. The name felt foreign on his tongue, like dust long forgotten in the back of his mind. His estranged grandfather, a man Black had only heard stories about. Stories filled with fire and brimstone, of battles fought not in courts but in streets, with fists and guns, with soldiers who feared no one but Allah.

Lion had once been a ranking member of the Black Sheep of Allah, a disgraced, disavowed offshoot of the Fruit of Islam's security force. They were men who had been cast out for being too extreme, too dangerous, for seeing every battle as one worth shedding blood over. If Black needed soldiers, Lion was the only one who could get them.

But the question wasn't if Lion could help—it was if he would. The two hadn't spoken in years, and Black had always known there would be a price to pay for asking this man for anything. Lion didn't do favors; he struck deals. Black would have to make it worthwhile. And that meant getting into bed with the devil himself.

The city blurred past as Black made his way to the address Pops had given him, a nondescript building tucked in the heart of a neighborhood that still wore its scars from battles long past. As he parked, Black felt the weight of what he was about to do settle in his chest.

Inside, the air was thick with the scent of incense and age. It was quiet—too quiet. Black stepped into a dimly lit room, his eyes adjusting to the shadowy figures seated around a long table. At the head, Lion Mohamed. His presence was as commanding as the legends had said—tall, broad, with a face carved by time and war, his eyes sharp, calculating.

"Black," Lion's voice cut through the silence, cold and distant. "What brings you to my door?"

Black stepped forward, meeting his grandfather's gaze without flinching. "I need help."

Lion didn't move, but his eyes flickered with a dangerous glint. "Help? You mean soldiers. Men who can do what you can't."

Black swallowed the lump in his throat, keeping his voice steady. "I need to level the playing field. I'm in the middle of something bigger than I realized, and I can't do it alone."

Lion leaned back, his fingers steepled together as he regarded Black with a mixture of amusement and caution. "And what do you offer me in return? Blood runs deep, but favors don't come cheap."

Black didn't hesitate. "A cut of what's coming. And if you play this right, a chance to reclaim what you lost. Respect."

Lion's lips curled into a slow, predatory smile. "Respect, you say? You think you can offer me something I already have?"

Black met his gaze, his voice low and firm. "I think I'm the only one who can get you what you want."

There was a beat of silence, heavy with unspoken threats. Then, Lion stood, his towering form casting a long shadow across the room.

"We'll see, boy. We'll see."

THIRTY-TWO

The drive back from Iowa was a long stretch of silence, the kind that clung to the car like fog, thick and impenetrable. The kind that gave a man too much time to think. Yehohanan had learned long ago that thoughts could be dangerous. They could unravel you if you weren't careful, turn quiet moments into storms brewing beneath the skin.

He glanced over at Professor Moore in the passenger seat. Her face was drawn, the edges of her profile etched with a weariness that went beyond exhaustion. She had held it together at the morgue, stiffened her spine and nodded when they asked her to identify her daughter's body. But now, with no one watching, he could see the cracks forming. Her hands were clenched in her lap, knuckles white from the grip. Her eyes, though fixed on the passing highway, were distant. Lost.

Yehohanan looked back at the road, his fingers tightening on the wheel. It was ironic, he thought, that the only reason he had walked free was because he'd once saved the life of Professor Moore's daughter. Years ago, behind bars, he'd traded his own safety to make sure she stayed alive, back when she was nothing more than a pawn in someone else's game. Now, here she was—cold, dead, and lying on a slab. And all he had to show for it was another body on his conscience.

The whole situation stank. From top to bottom.

Realistically, he had no reason to stick around. He wasn't tied to this mess, wasn't blood. Hell, Professor Moore had nothing left to hold him with except some vague notion of revenge and money. The former wasn't his style, and the latter, well... it wasn't looking too promising with the girl gone. But there was something else, something beneath it all that gnawed at him. A suspicion. Maybe Professor Moore had lied. Maybe she knew more than she let on.

Maybe she had the key code all along.

He glanced at her again. Her face was a mask, unreadable. She was good at that—keeping things locked up tight. But something about the way she had handled all this... it felt too controlled. Like she'd been waiting for this to happen. Not the death, but the shift. The way the world had turned on its axis, tilting the balance of power. And now, with her daughter dead, she held the cards. Or so she thought.

But Yehohanan wasn't sure if he was playing her game anymore. He'd seen men like her, seen how they twisted things when the heat was on. If she had lied about the code, then all bets were off. He'd walk, take what he could, and leave her to drown in the mess she'd made.

Still, there was the question of Sheek. He killed her, no doubt about it. Whether it was accidental or cold-blooded, Yehohanan couldn't say. But it didn't matter. Dead was dead. And now Sheek was deadlier than he'd anticipated. Killing the girl without getting the money? That was reckless, even for a man like Sheek. It meant one of two things: either Sheek had lost control, or he never cared about the money in the first place. And that was the kind of unpredictability Yehohanan didn't like.

He adjusted his grip on the wheel, his mind already working through the angles. The only advantage they had now was that Sheek didn't know they knew. The girl's death had bought them time, but not much. Sooner or later, he'd come looking for answers—or worse, for blood.

He could feel the clock ticking, a low hum in the back of his skull. They had no proof, but they didn't need it. Men like Sheek left a signature in everything they touched. It wasn't about evidence; it was about instinct. And Yehohanan's instincts were screaming that Sheek was coming for them next.

He flicked his eyes to the rearview mirror. The empty stretch of road behind them felt too open, too exposed. They'd need a plan, something fast and clean. Revenge wasn't going to be enough to survive this, and money—well, money wasn't going to get them out of the hole they were in.

Professor Moore shifted beside him, breaking the silence for the first time since the call from the Davenport detective. Her voice was hoarse, raw. "What now?"

Yehohanan kept his gaze straight ahead, his mind already moving three steps ahead. "We wait."

She frowned, turning to look at him, but he didn't elaborate. He didn't need to. The pieces were already in motion. Sheek had made his move, and now it was their turn.

But Yehohanan wasn't sure if he was ready to play the game she wanted him to. There were other ways out. Darker ways. He'd spent enough time in the gutter to know that sometimes, the only way to survive was to cut your losses and walk away. But not yet. Not until he knew what Professor Moore was hiding.

The car rumbled on, the highway stretching out before them like a promise. Or a warning.

Yehohanan couldn't tell which.

THIRTY-THREE

B lack sat in his car, the weight of his grandfather's words still pressing on him as he stared down at the burner phone in his hand. Lion had come through. The two soldiers on standby—Haidar and Nadiya Nova—were the best he could get on short notice. These weren't street thugs. They were professionals. Haidar, the cold-blooded former Marine Raider with a reputation for making bodies disappear in hostile territories, and Nadiya, a sharp-eyed IT specialist who could hack into places most people didn't even know existed.

Black wasn't a fool; he knew he was stepping into something bigger than a personal vendetta. This was war. But the battlefield had shifted, and every piece needed to be in place before the game exploded. He pocketed the phone and turned the key in the ignition. He had one more stop before things kicked off—Professor Moore's place.

As the engine rumbled to life, his mind flickered to the meeting earlier. Haidar and Nadiya had barely said a word when he laid out the plan. They understood the stakes, and that was enough. The silence was comfortable, the kind shared between people who didn't need to talk to understand each other. Haidar's quiet nod and

Nadiya's half-smile were all the confirmation Black needed. He had his mini-army. Now it was time to put them to use.

But something gnawed at him. A gut feeling. The kind you get when a shadow moves in the corner of your eye. He shook it off and focused on the road ahead. He had to keep his mind sharp. There was no room for mistakes.

When Black arrived at Professor Moore's apartment, the building was bathed in the dim, orange glow of streetlights. The city around him felt alive but distant, like a machine running quietly in the background. He parked across the street and made his way up the stairs, the faint smell of rain in the air. His mind was already racing through the next steps, contingency plans forming like puzzle pieces falling into place.

Professor Moore opened the door before he could knock. She looked exhausted, her eyes rimmed red from what was no doubt a lot of weeping. Her hands trembled as she stepped back to let him inside. The air in the apartment was thick, not just with tension, but with something darker. Loss. Grief.

"Thanks for coming," she muttered, trying to sound composed but failing miserably.

Black nodded, scanning the room out of habit. Nothing seemed out of place. He could hear Yehohanan in the other room, moving quietly like a shadow. The guy gave him the creeps, but Black respected his silence.

Moore sat down, clutching a glass of whiskey, the ice long since melted. "We need to move faster, Black. I'm running out of time."

He eyed her, not sure if she meant Sheek, or the thought of losing her daughter. Probably both. "Don't worry we're going to make it right."

"It's took late."

He raised an eyebrow. Looked at his watch. "He said he would give us time."

"He lied. She's dead. And I'm going to make sure he gets his."

"Wait a minute. Slow down. What happened?"

"Yehohanan and I just got back from Iowa, they found my baby there, strangled to death."

Black hung his head low. No words. he looked up, Moore looked at him, her expression unreadable.

The sound of a phone vibrating cut through the air. Her phone. She froze, her eyes locking onto it like it was a bomb about to go off. She picked it up slowly, her hands trembling worse now.

"Answer it," Black said, his voice low, steady.

She nodded and put the phone to her ear. "Hello?" Her face paled instantly, the color draining like someone had pulled a plug. Black's instincts kicked in, and he moved closer, listening. Black could feel the air shift, something dark and dangerous creeping in. Black's eyes narrowed. This wasn't good. Whoever was on the other end of that line knew something they shouldn't.

Moore hung up, her hand shaking so badly she nearly dropped the phone. She didn't speak, just sat there, her face contorted with grief and anger.

"What the hell happened?" Black asked, his voice tight.

"It's Sheek," she whispered, barely audible. "He knows we know, she's dead."

"Did he admit that it was him?"

She shook her head no. "No. But he still wants his money, he said figure out a way to get him his money, Bitcoin key pass or not he wants his money."

How did he know about the call from the Iowa police? Was his reach that far? For him to address the issue openly meant the situation was due to escalate sooner rather than later it meant he was already tightening the noose around their necks. Black began moving towards the door.

"Let's move." He said as he made his way into the hall and to the elevator followed closely by Professor Moore and Yehohanan. Now outside, Black's phone buzzed. It was Nadiya.

"Talk to me," he barked.

"There's chatter," she said, her voice calm but urgent. "Sheek's men are moving. Fast. They're coming for you."

Black's blood ran cold. This wasn't just about the money anymore. This was about survival.

"I'll handle it," Black snapped, ending the call. He turned to Moore, his expression hardening. "You need to leave. Now."

She was already shaking her head, her eyes wide with panic. "I can't—"

"You don't have a choice," Black cut in, his voice sharp.

"I won't!"

"We don't have time for this." Yehohanan says, more urgently than expected.

"We have to move."

"Inside." Yehohanan says as he points up the street to a caravan of cars speeding in their direction.

The trio backs back into the building.

"Was it just me or was that a shit load of cars?" Yehohanan says, looking through the window on the door as the cars pile into the parking lot. They head to the elevator to find that it is out of order.

Black's phone buzzes again. Nadiya. "Just got word, there's a bounty on you all ten thousand a head. Forty even if all brought in alive."

"You've got to be kidding me."

"That's not the worst part."

Black laughed sarcastically. "Oh do tell."

"Sheek has connections, half the squad cars in this area have been diverted to the other side of town and the other half have been ordered to stop all traffic from coming or going in from 89th and Jeffery to 94th- 94th and Stony to Colfax back up to 89th no one in or out."

"They boxed us in"

"Every hitter in the city is coming for that money, no police interference it's open season. Haidar is on his way, he can get in, just stay alive until he gets there."

"Anything else?"

"Yeah, if I were them, I would block the cell towers so you couldn't make calls-" The call went dead. Black looked at his phone and slid it back in his pocket.

He turned to Professor Moore, her face illuminated by the weak light from the emergency exit sign. She looked up at him, her eyes wide with terror, her breathing shallow. Yehohanan stood behind her, his eyes hard and focused, but even he seemed aware of how close they were to the edge.

Black's mind raced. They had to stall, buy themselves enough time for Nadiya and Haidar to arrive. But Sheek's men were too many, too prepared. This wasn't just a bounty hunt—it was a lockdown. He knew the minute those goons outside got bored or impatient, they'd storm the building, guns blazing.

He leaned closer to Moore, his voice barely a whisper. "We don't have time for mistakes. You sure you've told me everything?"

She swallowed, her hands shaking as she clenched them into fists. "I told you... everything." But there was something in her voice, a hesitation, a crack in the façade.

Black's eyes narrowed. "You better not be lying. We're already deep in the shit."

She didn't respond, but her gaze dropped to the floor, her silence speaking louder than words.

Suddenly, the building's power flickered. The dull hum of the lights overhead sputtered before plunging them into near darkness, save for the emergency lights still glowing faintly in the stairwell. The unmistakable sound of someone cutting the power.

"They're coming." Yehohanan's voice was cold, emotionless. He stood by the door, listening for footsteps, his body coiled like a predator ready to strike.

Black's jaw clenched. They were running out of time, and there were too many unknowns. He could feel it—the walls closing in, the noose tightening. He couldn't afford to wait for Nadiya and Haidar. They needed a plan, now.

THIRTY-FOUR

B lack could hear the echo of footsteps pounding up the stairwell behind them, the sounds of pursuit closing in like the jaws of a hungry beast. The flickering emergency lights cast long shadows on the concrete walls, painting everything in shades of danger. Professor Moore was ahead of him, breathing hard but still moving, and Yehohanan, cold and methodical as ever, brought up the rear.

The plan to reach the roof and jump from building to building was desperate—insane even—but it was the only shot they had left. If they could get high enough and stay in the shadows, they might be able to disappear into the night, leaving Sheek's assassins to search the empty halls for ghosts. But before they could even think about that, they had to fight their way back down, floor by floor, through a gauntlet of hired killers.

They burst through the door to the next floor, finding themselves in a long corridor lined with office spaces. The hum of fluorescent lights buzzed overhead, giving the place an eerie, abandoned feel. Black's mind flashed to the sound of gunfire and the faces of men who were probably already on the floor below, closing in.

"Keep moving," Black said, his voice a harsh whisper as they raced down the hallway. His fingers curled around the grip of his gun, his senses on high alert. This was no ordinary escape. It was a warzone, and every step felt like a gamble with death.

Just as they approached the stairwell at the far end of the hall, the door burst open. Three men stepped through—each of them armed and ready, their eyes gleaming with the cold efficiency of professionals. One of them, a tall man with a scar across his face, smirked.

"Going somewhere?" he sneered, raising his gun.

Without hesitation, Black shoved Professor Moore to the side and fired. The gunshots echoed off the walls, the bright flash of the muzzle lighting up the dark corridor like lightning. The scar-faced man went down, his body collapsing with a thud, but his partners reacted instantly, returning fire with deadly precision.

The group dove for cover as bullets whizzed past, slamming into the walls and shattering glass. Black's heart pounded in his chest, the adrenaline pushing him into overdrive. He glanced at Yehohanan, who was crouched behind an overturned desk, his face calm, almost eerily so.

"We can't stay here!" Black shouted, pulling Moore closer as more shots rang out. "We have to keep moving."

Yehohanan nodded, then leaped from his hiding spot, his body a blur of motion. In a flash, he was on one of the gunmen, taking him down with brutal efficiency. The crack of bones echoed through the narrow corridor, and the man hit the ground like a sack of bricks. But before Black could react, the final assassin aimed squarely at Yehohanan, his finger tightening on the trigger.

"Yehohanan!" Black roared, already pulling his weapon up to fire again. But it was Moore who acted first, swinging a fire extinguisher she'd grabbed from the wall, crashing it into the man's head with a sickening thud. The killer went down in a heap, unconscious.

Yehohanan looked up, his eyes cold and unreadable, but there was a flicker of acknowledgment in them as he nodded at Moore. She was shaking but stood her ground, breath heavy, the fire extinguisher still clutched in her hands like a lifeline.

"Let's move!" Black barked, pulling them all toward the stairwell.

They raced down the stairs, every creak and groan of the old building adding to the tension. As they reached the next landing, Black could hear the muffled voices of more men below, likely lying in wait, their footsteps echoing up the stairwell.

"We're boxed in," Moore whispered, her voice trembling.

"Not yet," Black said, his mind working at a frantic pace. "We take them out one by one. No mistakes."

They moved in tight formation—Yehohanan leading, Black in the middle, Moore in the rear. The sound of their pursuers grew louder as they approached the next door. Black could feel the sweat trickling down his neck, his muscles tensed, ready for the fight that was bound to come.

Yehohanan reached the door first, cracking it open just enough to peer through. He turned back to Black and nodded once—a silent signal. Without a word, they burst through.

The room was a storage area, dimly lit and crammed with boxes. Three more of Sheek's men were waiting for them. The moment the door flew open, the air exploded with violence.

Yehohanan moved first, a blur of motion as he closed the distance between himself and the closest gunman. A brutal elbow to the throat took the man down in seconds, but there was no time to admire the efficiency. Black fired at the second gunman, his shot hitting the man in the shoulder, sending him spinning into the wall.

The third man lunged at Moore, a knife glinting in the dim light. She screamed, stumbling back, but Black was there in an instant, firing a round into the man's chest. The attacker crumpled to the ground, his body twitching as life drained out of him.

The room was quiet now, except for the sound of ragged breathing. They were alive—for now.

"We're running out of time," Yehohanan said, his voice steady but urgent. "More will be coming."

Black wiped sweat from his brow, his mind racing. "We have to get to the roof. That's our only chance."

They pushed on, the stairwell creaking beneath their feet as they ascended. But when they reached the top floor, another group of Sheek's assassins was waiting for them, blocking the door to the roof.

Black cursed under his breath. They were trapped.

"This is it," he said, glancing at Moore and Yehohanan. "No more running. We fight our way through."

Yehohanan nodded, his eyes like ice. Moore swallowed hard, gripping her fire extinguisher as if it were her last defense.

The assassins charged.

Black fired first, the sound of gunshots deafening in the narrow space. The chaos of battle erupted, fists and bullets flying as they fought for their lives. Each move felt like a gamble, each breath a test of endurance.

But they were outnumbered, and the pressure was mounting. Black took down one man with a well-aimed shot, but another tackled him, sending them both crashing into the stairwell wall. The impact jarred Black, but he fought back, grappling with the assassin as the two men struggled for control.

Yehohanan was a storm of violence, taking down men with ruthless efficiency. But even he was slowing, the endless wave of attackers pushing them to their limits.

Moore swung her extinguisher wildly, barely fending off another assassin as the room closed in around them.

Suddenly, a gunshot rang out from behind them.

Black turned, blood running cold as he saw Moore fall to the ground, clutching her side. Time seemed to slow as he rushed to her side, his heart pounding in his chest.

"Moore!" he shouted, but there was no time for hesitation.

The assassins were closing in, and Haidar was still nowhere to be found.

With no other choice, Black grabbed Moore, slinging her arm over his shoulder as Yehohanan covered their retreat.

They had to make it to the roof. It was their only chance.

THIRTY-FIVE

Black and his makeshift team moved down the dim hallway, their footsteps heavy, desperation hanging in the air like a noose. They knocked frantically on every door, hoping, praying, that someone inside might help. But every door remained shut. The walls were as silent as the people behind them, all unwilling to be dragged into whatever deadly game had spilled into their building.

Professor Moore was bleeding more now, her face pale, her breath coming in shallow gasps. It was looking bleak—no help, no escape, and only a matter of time before Sheek's men caught up. The footsteps behind them echoed in the stairwell, growing louder, closer. Black was almost out of ammo. His mind raced, calculating how much longer they could last. Not long.

"We gotta move," Black muttered, his voice tight, eyes scanning the hall.

They decided to head back to the stairwell, their best hope of getting to the roof and jumping to the next building. Black's body ached, but he pushed through it, adrenaline keeping him on edge. Yehohanan opened the stairwell door, leading the way, followed by Black and a limping Professor Moore. Just as they entered, they froze. The sound of heavy footsteps echoed up from below. A man with a gun came into view, walking toward them slowly, deliberately, a deadly confidence in his steps.

"Back up," Black whispered, his voice barely audible.

They started to retreat, moving cautiously, but before the gunman could fully step through the door, a sharp, sickening *crack* echoed in the tight space. Blood splattered against the wall as the man crumpled to the floor, a gaping wound in his head.

Black, Moore, and Yehohanan spun around, eyes wide, ready for another attack, but what they found was a man standing over the body, a bloodied cricket bat resting on his shoulder.

"I don't like the numbers in this match," the man said with a thick Nigerian accent, his voice steady and casual, as if this were just another day at the office. "Thought I'd join the underdog team."

He spun the cricket bat in his hands with a smooth, practiced motion, the blood staining the wood almost blending in with the dark varnish.

"Thanks for the solid," Black said, giving the man a quick pat on the back, still processing the strange encounter.

The man shot Professor Moore a knowing look, his dark eyes gleaming with something like recognition. "Are you sure you want help from a damn foreigner?" he asked, his words laced with something heavier, more personal.

Black looked confused, glancing between the two. Yehohanan's face tightened, as if he suddenly understood something that had been simmering beneath the surface. Professor Moore, however, looked embarrassed, her eyes darting away, refusing to meet Chioma's gaze.

But Black had no time for awkward moments or personal grudges. "Let's move," he said, urgency creeping into his voice. "Chioma, my brother, grab his piece." He gestured to the gun on the floor.

Chioma shook his head, smiling as he kissed the bloody cricket bat. "All I need is this. Nigeria Cricket Federation—best in the world, baby." He kissed the logo again with pride, the wild glint in his eyes suggesting he was more than ready for what came next.

Yehohanan, ever practical, scooped up the dead man's gun without hesitation and nodded toward the stairwell. They started moving again, descending into the darkness below. The air grew thicker with every step, the weight of what was coming pressing down on all of them. Black's senses were sharp, his mind in overdrive. Every sound, every creak in the building seemed louder now.

Suddenly, the stairwell vibrated with the sound of more footsteps—heavier this time, deliberate. Another squad of Sheek's men, closing in fast.

"We're blocked," Yehohanan said, eyeing the obstruction that now barred their way to the roof. It was a barricade, hastily set up by Sheek's men. They'd expected this. Black cursed under his breath.

"We're going back down," Black growled, his voice low, controlled. "Fight our way out."

They descended the stairs quickly, but not fast enough. The door below them burst open, and three more gunmen stormed in. Black didn't hesitate. He rushed forward, firing the last of his ammo in quick succession, hitting one man square in the chest, sending him crashing into the railing. The second man raised his gun, but before he could pull the trigger, Black was on him.

With a swift, brutal motion, Black grabbed the man by the collar, smashing his face against the concrete wall. The man groaned, dropping his weapon as blood poured from his nose. Black finished him with a hard elbow to the temple, the force of it knocking him out cold.

Chioma, grinning wildly, stepped in as the third man lunged at him. With a smooth, fluid motion, he swung the cricket bat, connecting with the man's ribcage with a sickening crack. The man screamed, but before he could fall, Chioma swung again, the bat connecting with his skull this time. The man's body hit the floor, twitching violently as the life drained out of him.

"Best in the world!" Chioma shouted, his voice filled with a kind of manic joy as he spun the bat in his hands, ready for more.

But Black wasn't celebrating. His chest was heaving, his mind racing. There was no time to rest, no time to take stock. They had to keep moving.

Another group was already flooding the stairwell, their heavy footsteps growing louder, closer.

Black turned, eyes scanning the space. "Get ready," he said, his voice low and deadly. This wasn't over—not by a long shot. The fight was just beginning.

The next wave hit hard. Black was at the front, fists and elbows moving like machines, precise and brutal. He felt the crack of bone against his knuckles as he delivered punch after punch, but he couldn't stop. One man went down, then another, but more kept coming, their faces twisted with a hunger for blood and the bounty on their heads.

Moore, barely hanging on, slumped against the wall, her breath coming in ragged gasps. Yehohanan fired shot after shot, covering Black as best he could. Chioma, still grinning like a madman, swung his cricket bat wildly, taking down any man who came too close.

They were fighting for their lives now, no rules, no mercy.

THIRTY-SIX

The stairwell reeked of sweat and blood, every step reverberating with the echo of bodies hitting concrete. Black moved cautiously, his Glock clenched tight in his grip, his eyes scanning the shadows. They had made it down two flights of stairs, but each step was a new battle—more thugs, more chaos.

Yehohanan was at the front now, leading the charge. His eyes were cold, calculating as he moved through the narrow space with surgical precision. With each hit, he seemed to grow more focused, his breathing steady even as bodies piled up around them. A knife flashed in his hand, cutting through the throat of a man charging from the left. One quick slash, and the guy crumpled without a sound. Black couldn't help but feel a grudging respect. The man was deadly, no doubt about it.

Chioma followed close behind, his cricket bat in hand. He swung it with a kind of joy, the wooden weapon splintering bones, sending attackers crashing into walls. Every time the bat made contact, there was a sickening crack, but Chioma's grin never wavered.

The door to the next landing burst open, and two more men rushed them. Yehohanan ducked low, moving in a blur, his knife finding its mark in one of the men's ribs. Chioma stepped forward, driving the bat into the other man's chest with a bone-shattering crunch.

For a moment, the stairwell was quiet again, the only sound their ragged breathing.

They rested against the railing, catching their breath as the carnage settled around them. Moore was leaning heavily against the wall, her face pale, her breaths coming in short gasps. She wouldn't last much longer.

"How you holding up?" Black asked, his voice low but steady, though he knew the answer.

Moore barely nodded, her hand pressed against her side, blood soaking through her fingers.

Chioma, still gripping his bat, sat down on the steps, his grin fading slightly as the adrenaline wore off. Black looked at him, finally curious about the man who had appeared out of nowhere.

"You move well for a guy with a cricket bat," Black said, wiping the blood from his own face. "What's your story?"

Chioma chuckled, leaning back against the stairwell wall, his breathing slowing. "Long story, but we got a few minutes between fights, don't we?"

Black didn't say anything, just gave him a look that said, "Talk."

Chioma spun the bat in his hand, almost absentmindedly. "Name's Chioma Musa Ibrahim. Born in the Republic of Benin. I've always been a bit of a drifter, you know? My father, though, was from Harlem. Worked for the Secret Service—met my mother during a UN meeting in Nigeria. It's funny, they gave me my mom's last name just to make life easier for me over there. You'd think being American-born would be a benefit, but in Nigeria, a foreigner's name can be more trouble than it's worth."

Black nodded, taking in the story as Chioma continued, his voice calm despite the situation.

"I bounced around growing up. Spent time in Italy, Spain, wherever my old man got posted. Played sports—whatever I could get into. Calcio Storico was my thing, though. Rough sport. Not much for rules, which suits me just fine."

"You play in Italy?" Black asked, his brow raised, genuinely surprised.

"Yeah," Chioma grinned, wiping the blood from his bat with his sleeve. "In Florence. That game's no joke, man. It's like a mix of rugby, soccer, and a street fight. Been a lot of places, seen a lot of things. Guess that's why when I saw you three in a mess, I couldn't resist joining. Figured the odds were stacked against you."

Black gave a slight nod, respect flashing in his eyes for a second before his face hardened again. "Appreciate it," he muttered, though he didn't have time for pleasantries. Not here, not now.

Chioma shrugged. "Always liked backing the underdog, you know?"

Before Black could respond, his phone buzzed in his pocket. He pulled it out, checking the screen—Nadiya.

He answered, stepping away slightly from the group. "Talk to me," he said, his voice tense.

Her voice came through with a calm confidence that Black had come to rely on. "Tapped into the network, Black. I got the cell towers back online for the area. "Black," Nadiya's voice was calm, controlled. "Haidar's on the premises. He's not inside the building yet, but he's on standby. Ready to give cover when you make it out."

Black felt a brief surge of relief, but it was fleeting. "Understood. The other thing. You get it done?"

There was a brief pause, the sound of her tapping on a keyboard before she answered, cryptic as ever. "It's in motion. You'll know when it happens."

Black frowned, wanting more, but he knew better than to push. "And the other part?"

A longer pause this time. "Consider it handled."

Before he could ask more, the line went dead. Black slipped the phone back into his pocket, a sense of unease creeping in, but now wasn't the time for questions. He'd have to trust her for now.

Black grunted. He pocketed the phone and turned back to the group. "Haidar's outside. We just need to get out of this building."

Yehohanan nodded. "Then let's stop wasting time." He was already moving, checking the stairwell below for more enemies.

Black took point, his mind sharp, adrenaline pumping again. Chioma moved alongside him, and Black couldn't help but appreciate the man's casual confidence. They were an odd team, but right now, they were all he had.

"Keep your head straight," Black muttered to Moore as they moved toward the next flight of stairs. "We're almost there."

But they all knew it was only going to get worse from here.

Thirty-Seven

D rake rolled up to the warehouse on the west side, the engine of his car purring to a stop. It was the kind of place deals got done without handshakes, where shadows swallowed the light and men disappeared just as easily as money changed hands. The air was heavy, thick with the scent of exhaust and wet concrete. Drake stepped out, adjusting his jacket, eyes darting around the dimly lit lot. His heart was drumming in his chest, but not from fear. Anticipation coursed through him like adrenaline. This was his moment.

Inside, the warehouse was a cavern of silence, the only sound the soft hum of industrial lights flickering above. The kind of light that barely cut through the gloom, casting long shadows that seemed to stretch endlessly. Drake's footsteps echoed across the concrete floor as he approached a group of men near a stack of crates. They were the crew Malik had connected him with—Detroit muscle with enough clout to push the kind of weight Drake needed to flip the game.

Jace, a heavyset man with a jawline as sharp as his temper, watched Drake approach. His arms crossed over his broad chest, eyes narrowed beneath the brim of his cap.

"You're late," Jace growled, his voice as rough as gravel.

Drake flashed a tight smile, the kind that didn't quite reach his eyes. "Traffic."

Jace grunted, unimpressed, then jerked his head toward the duffel bag Drake was carrying. "The sample you promised, I assume?"

Drake tossed the bag near his feet. Jace knelt, unzipped the bag and peered inside. Zipped it back closed and stood.

Drake opened his mouth to respond, but a sound from the far end of the warehouse cut him off—a creaking door, slow and deliberate. Drake's stomach clenched as he turned toward the noise. A figure stepped through the doorway, backlit by the faint glow of a streetlight behind them. Tall. Calm. Dressed head to toe in black, moving with the kind of confidence that made the world pause.

The shadows peeled away, and there he was.

Sheek.

The room seemed to close in on Drake, the air thickening, suffocating. Sheek moved with the ease of a predator, his steps measured, his face shrouded in cold indifference. The faint echo of his footsteps filled the space, and suddenly, everything else—the crates, Jace, the deal—faded into the background.

Drake's breath caught in his throat. How had Sheek known?

"Sheek—" Drake started, his voice tighter than he intended, but Sheek's cold eyes silenced him before the words could find air.

"You've been busy, Drake," Sheek said, his voice a low rumble, smooth like silk but with the weight of iron beneath it. He stepped closer, his gaze never leaving Drake, pinning him like a predator sizing up its prey.

Drake's pulse raced, the walls of the warehouse seeming to close in on him. His mind scrambled for something—an excuse, an explanation, anything to slow the train wreck that was about to unfold. Jace and his crew stood still, their faces neutral, betraying nothing. It hit Drake then—the deal had been a setup from the start. The betrayal hung in the air, thick and suffocating. He'd been played.

"I can explain—" Drake stammered, but Sheek raised a hand, cutting him off with the simple gesture of a man who owned everything in the room.

"You think I didn't know?" Sheek's voice was barely above a whisper now, yet it carried the weight of an executioner's verdict. He stepped closer, his gaze boring into Drake's. "You thought you could move weight in my city, with my people, and I wouldn't find out?"

Drake swallowed hard, his throat dry, his mind racing but coming up with nothing. "It's not what it looks like-"

Sheek took another step forward, his presence consuming the space around them. The air crackled with the unspoken threat, each second stretching longer than the last.

"This is my city," Sheek growled, his voice a low rumble that sent a shiver down Drake's spine. "And I don't care how many deals you think you can make."

Drake felt the vise tighten. Every option he thought he had, every move he'd planned, was slipping away. The weight of Sheek's power pressed down on him, squeezing the life out of the air. This wasn't a negotiation. This was the end.

"I—" Drake began again, but his words were cut short by the flash of Sheek's hand.

A gunshot cracked through the warehouse like thunder. Drake stumbled, his hand instinctively flying to his chest as the burning pain seared through him. He fell to his knees, gasping for breath as the blood spread quickly through his shirt, dark and warm against the cold concrete.

Sheek crouched down next to him, his face calm, almost serene. He leaned in close, his voice a whisper that cut deeper than the bullet. "You should've known better."

Drake's vision blurred, the edges of the world growing dim. His breath came in shallow gasps as he looked up into Sheek's cold, unfeeling eyes. The last thing he saw before everything went dark was Sheek standing tall, wiping his hands clean of the mess.

Sheek turned to Jace and the others, his voice calm and measured as ever. "Get rid of this. Let the city know— it was me."

"What about his connect?"

"I'll deal with his connect, we have history." And with that, Sheek walked away, his footsteps echoing through the vast, empty warehouse, his empire still intact. Untouchable.

THIRTY-EIGHT

Black kept his pace steady as they descended the final flight of stairs, Professor Moore trailing behind, her breaths shallow, her mind clearly elsewhere. The adrenaline had dulled her wounds, but the pain lingered in her eyes, haunted and empty. She muttered something under her breath, words caught in a tangle of regret.

"This was all for nothing," she whispered, almost to herself. "It was supposed to be my happy ending."

Black glanced back, barely catching the words. "What are you babbling about?" he asked, his tone sharp. He didn't have time for riddles.

Moore shook her head, dismissing it. "Never mind."

Black let out a dark chuckle, his voice echoing off the cold concrete walls. "Happily ever after, huh? You and Drake, right?" He shot her a knowing glance, waiting for the inevitable reaction.

She froze for a moment, eyes narrowing as if she'd been caught in a lie she hadn't even meant to tell. But she didn't respond, just clenched her jaw and kept moving.

Black smirked. "That's alright, you don't have to admit it. I already know." His voice dropped lower, more menacing. "If you die now—which, honestly, I should just finish you off—it would be the scales balancing, wouldn't it?"

Moore's silence was louder than any denial. She didn't look at him, didn't say a word. She just kept walking, her focus on the ground in front of her.

"Execution's not my style, though," Black continued, almost thoughtful. "So, I'm not going to do it."

"Save the moral high ground, Black," Moore snapped, her voice brittle. "I don't want to hear it. I've lost everything."

Black shook his head slowly. "No," he said, "not everything."

"Perspective," she shot back bitterly.

He raised an eyebrow, half-impressed. "Touche."

For a moment, the only sound was their footsteps, heavy and slow. The weight of the truth, of all the lies and schemes, hung between them like a thick fog.

"Make this right, Professor," Black said, his tone turning colder. "I know you didn't come up with this dumbass plan. And I know it wasn't Drake. He's even dumber than you."

She shot him a glare, but the insult didn't faze her. They both knew the truth.

"What are you asking me?" Her voice was tense now, guarded.

"I'm asking you to tell me who orchestrated all of this. Or this is where our ride together ends." He stopped and turned to face her, his eyes hard, unyielding. "You'll have to make it out of here on your own."

Moore hesitated, her breath catching in her throat. The seconds stretched on, the decision weighing heavily on her shoulders. She looked up at Black, her face a mask of pain, desperation, and, finally, defeat.

"It was Malik," she said, the words falling out in a rush. "I don't know why, but he has a vendetta against Sheek. He put all the moving parts together, even placed your secretary in my class, so when I came to you, it would seem more... *organic*."

Black's gaze stayed locked on her, unreadable. But inside, gears were turning.

Moore's voice cracked as she finished. "I didn't want this."

Black watched her, his expression softening slightly, though his eyes remained sharp. "Thanks for telling me the truth."

They both knew the stakes had shifted, but the game wasn't over yet. Not even close.

THIRTY-NINE

Lerone "Hambone" Berber had been an institution in Chicago politics long before Black ever crossed his path. A crooked Alderman who knew how to pull strings from the shadows, Hambone was the kind of man who thrived in chaos, using the city's underbelly to keep his hands greased and his pockets lined. He had ties to everyone—from the mob to the mayor's office—because he never turned down a deal, so long as it benefited him.

Black and Hambone first crossed paths a few weeks ago, forced together through circumstance it ended being beneficial for both. The two of them struck an uneasy alliance, built on mutual gain and quiet understanding—if you scratched Hambone's back, he'd make sure the system looked the other way. But you never forgot the cost. Black needed access and cover. It wasn't friendship, but in their world, survival meant having people like Hambone in your corner.

As Black moved down the stairwell, he knew exactly who he had to call.

Letting the others move ahead, he pulled out his burner and dialed Hambone's number. The phone rang twice before the familiar gravelly voice answered.

"Who the hell is this?" Hambone growled, his voice thick with disdain, like he hadn't been woken up for anything less than life or death.

"It's Black," he replied, keeping his voice low. "I've got a deal for you."

A pause. Then the sound of a drag on a cigarette, the ember crackling on the other end. "Oh, this oughta be good. What's the play?"

"I need some favors," Black cut straight to it. "There's a blockade. Unsanctioned. Cops have the area locked down, no one in or out. I need that lifted. Fast."

Hambone let out a deep, knowing chuckle. "You've got a knack for gettin' into shit, don't you, Black? What's in it for me?"

"Money. Enough to spread around and keep some pockets happy. Plus, I'll owe you one. A big one."

Another drag, followed by a long exhale. "A favor from Black Love? That's rare stock. But I don't work on promises. I need something more...immediate."

Black smirked to himself. Typical Hambone. "You help me, and I'll give you something extra—a bonus. Call it a thank you."

The line went silent for a moment, the Alderman's mind clearly working the angles. Hambone was sharp. Too sharp to let a potential payday slip by, but always calculating risk. "Bonus, huh? And what might that be?"

"Details after the job's done," Black replied smoothly. "You lift the blockade, and my people outside will reach out to you with the particulars."

Hambone chewed on that for a beat. The old man knew cutting ties with Black wouldn't just dry up a reliable source of side income—it'd mean losing a valuable player in his back pocket. The kind of person who could fix things when they went sideways. And Hambone had more enemies than friends.

"All right," Hambone grunted. "But if this backfires, the heat's on you, not me. I'll make some calls."

Black glanced up the stairwell. "Just make sure it happens fast. We're running on borrowed time."

Hambone's voice sharpened. "Yeah, yeah. Don't tell me how to do my job. I'll take care of it. But remember—you owe me, and I don't let debts go unpaid."

Black's grin was cold. "Make it happen Hambone."

With a click, the call ended, and Black pocketed the phone. He took a breath, eyes scanning the stairwell as the weight of the situation pressed down on him. The blockade would be lifted soon—at least now there was a crack in the police cordon. But getting out alive was still going to take more than just a favor from a crooked Alderman.

He pushed off the wall and headed to rejoin the others.

One problem down. A thousand more to go.

FORTY

Sheek slid into the backseat of his blacked-out SUV, the scent of leather mingling with the lingering smell of gunpowder and sweat from the night's events. The warehouse deal had gone down like clockwork, and yet there was a gnawing unease that clung to the air around him. His driver, Marcus, gave him a quick nod in the rearview mirror before turning his attention back to the road.

"Where to, boss?" Marcus asked.

"Drive," Sheek said, his voice low, controlled.

As the SUV rolled through the shadowed streets, the faint hum of the city barely audible through the thick, bulletproof glass, Sheek's eyes fell on something that shouldn't have been there—a laptop, sleek and unfamiliar, resting on the seat beside him. His brow furrowed. That wasn't his.

He picked it up, running a thumb over the lid before glancing toward Marcus. "Where'd this come from?"

Marcus didn't turn around, just kept his eyes on the road. "No idea, boss. Didn't see anyone put it in."

Sheek narrowed his gaze, his gut instinct screaming that this wasn't a mistake. He flipped the laptop open, a soft click echoing through the silent interior. The screen flickered to life immediately. No password. No security. Just a simple interface with a single video file. A flash drive was plugged into the side—an anonymous gift, one he hadn't asked for.

With one click, the video began to play.

The screen lit up with a face Sheek hadn't seen in years but would recognize anywhere—Malik. His older brother. The one who had vanished into the background, content to leave Sheek in the spotlight, or so he'd thought.

Malik's face was calm, his expression cold, as if they were about to sit down for a casual conversation instead of what was clearly a message laced with venom. The video crackled with the faint sound of background noise, wind whipping against the mic as Malik leaned in, a sardonic smile tugging at his lips.

"Well played, Sheek," Malik's voice was a smooth, measured drawl, the kind of tone that could lull you into a false sense of security. "I'll give you that. You beat me this time. But that's not why I'm here."

Sheek's jaw tightened. His grip on the laptop grew firmer as Malik's words washed over him, a sinister chill creeping up his spine.

"I've been watching from the shadows long enough. And to be honest, little brother, I got bored. It's not fun letting you win if you don't even know I'm playing."

Sheek's lips curled into a sneer, his eyes narrowing at the screen.

Malik's smile grew wider, his eyes gleaming with a dark, twisted amusement. "But now? Now it'll be more fun. Because you see, Sheek, I'm stepping out of the shadows. I want you to know it's me coming for you. I want you to see it all unravel before your eyes."

The SUV hit a slight bump, but Sheek barely noticed. He was too focused on the screen, on the words dripping with venom and cold precision. This wasn't just a taunt. It was a declaration of war.

"It's been a long time coming, hasn't it?" Malik continued, his voice taking on a more menacing edge. "But here's the best part—I'm giving you a chance. I could've stayed hidden, could've let you keep running things, never knowing who was pulling the strings. But where's the fun in that?"

The video flickered, Malik leaning closer to the camera, his eyes locking onto the lens like he was staring directly into Sheek's soul.

"I'm telling you now because I want you to sweat. I want you to look over your shoulder every second of every day, knowing that the end is coming. From me."

The silence in the SUV was thick, oppressive, as Malik's final words lingered in the air.

"Good luck, little brother."

The video cut off, the screen going black.

Sheek sat in the backseat, the glow of the city lights casting faint shadows over his face, his expression unreadable. The cold edge of Malik's message settled into his bones, but instead of anger, a slow, sinister smile spread across his lips.

Malik thought he could step out of the shadows and challenge him? Thought he could come for the throne? He should've stayed hidden. He should've stayed safe in the dark, because now, with Malik in the light, Sheek had a target.

He closed the laptop, the weight of it now a distant thought as his mind began to churn. There was no panic, no fear. Just calculation. Malik wanted a game? Sheek would give him one. But this time, there wouldn't be any rules. No safety nets. No shadows to hide in.

The sinister smile deepened as he spoke quietly, more to himself than to Marcus. "He made his move."

Marcus glanced in the mirror, unsure of what had just happened. "Everything good, boss?"

Sheek's eyes flickered, the cold gleam of a man who had just been given a reason to kill. "Oh, it's perfect."

He leaned back in the seat, his fingers tapping lightly against the closed laptop. Malik wanted a challenge, but Sheek wasn't just going to win—he was going to destroy everything his brother ever touched.

The empire wasn't just going to remain intact. It was going to grow, thrive, while Malik crumbled beneath its weight. And when the time came, Sheek would be there, watching, savoring every moment as his brother realized just how outmatched he really was.

The car rolled on through the night, the city outside continuing as if nothing had changed. But for Sheek, everything had. The game had just begun. And he was about to show Malik exactly why you never, ever challenged the king.

FORTY-ONE

B lack had re-taken the lead, moving like a shadow through the final stretch of the stairwell. His breath was steady, but his mind raced. The weight of the night pressed on him, and he knew they were running out of time. Reaching the exit, he peered through the cracked door, eyes narrowing as he took in the scene outside. Lines of cars, parked haphazardly, blocked the street, while clusters of men stood by, guarding the entrance like vultures waiting for the kill.

Black's phone buzzed in his pocket, a jarring reminder of reality. He glanced down at the screen—Nadiya. "The blockade's lifted," her voice crackled through. "And the deal with the Alderman is in motion."

He breathed out a low grunt of approval. "Good. But the bounty's still out there. Stay sharp," he muttered, more to himself than to her.

"One more thing," she added. "Haidar's in position. He'll cover you when you make your move."

Black ended the call and turned to the others. His eyes flicked over the ragtag group—Professor Moore, wounded and pale, Chioma, with his cricket bat in hand, and Yehohanan, cold and silent as always. "Blockade's down," he said. "But the bounty's still on. Stay alert."

They exchanged glances, each of them knowing the stakes. Before they could move, the distant wail of sirens pierced the night air, echoing down the narrow alleyways like a warning. The police were closing in, but they weren't the ones Black was worried about. As he nudged the door open, stepping out into the cool night, the first shot rang out. Black saw a flash of movement—a man raising his gun—then the top of his head exploded, his body crumpling like a marionette with its strings cut.

Another shot. Another body hit the ground. But no one had fired from their group. Black kept his cool, his eyes scanning the rooftops, the dark corners. Haidar's handiwork, no doubt. But then, as the rest of the men outside scrambled for cover, three figures emerged from the crowd. These ones were different. No guns. No hesitation. They moved as if they had nothing to lose.

Black held up a hand, signaling for Haidar to hold his fire. The three men closed in, calm and collected, like wolves circling their prey. Black stepped forward, taking the lead, meeting their eyes with a steady, measured gaze.

The man in the center—thick build, tattoos creeping up his neck like vines—stopped a few feet away. "Tell me," he said, his voice dripping with disdain, "why I shouldn't blow your head off right now."

Black gave a slow shrug, his tone cold. "Because you wouldn't make it out of here alive."

The man's lips curled into a smirk. "Maybe I would, maybe I wouldn't."

He glanced over Black's shoulder, sizing up the group. "Strange little crew you got here," he said. "Wounded old woman, an African, and a white boy with a face full of prison ink." He sneered at Yehohanan, who remained still, his gaze steady.

Yehohanan stepped forward, his eyes narrowing at the man's tattoos. He pointed at the Star of David and the trident inked into the man's skin. "That tattoo. I've seen it before."

The man scowled. "Yeah, and? You've seen a Disciple tattoo before, white boy?"

Yehohanan shook his head slowly, his voice low. "Nah. The one under it." He pointed again, this time at a tattoo of a woman's face next to two young boys. "You related to Cans?"

The man stiffened, his bravado faltering. "Who?"

"Cans. Ran the block inside. Got a tattoo just like that. You his brother?"

The man's face darkened. He fumbled for his phone, dialing a number with shaky hands. After a few rings, someone answered. The man kept his eyes on Yehohanan, his voice tense. "Yeah, I don't know if it's a good time or not, bro, but there's this big country-looking white boy here. Says he knows you. Calls himself Yehohanan."

He listened for a few seconds, his expression hardening. Then, slowly, he nodded. "Yeah, he's got some people with him. Should I give them a pass or not?"

Another pause. The man glanced at Yehohanan, then back at the phone. "Alright. Be careful in there, bro. I'll have Ma call you at seven."

He ended the call, his demeanor shifting. "My brother says you're a stand-up guy. So, you and your people get a pass. For now."

With that, he turned on his heel, motioning for his men to follow. They climbed into their cars and disappeared into the night, just as the police sirens grew louder, cutting through the tension like a knife.

A black Suburban rolled up next to the group. Black instinctively tensed, but when the door opened, it wasn't a threat—it was the Chief of Police. The man stepped out, his face grim, his eyes locking onto Black. "This is a shitstorm," he muttered, shaking his head. "Give my officers your names and numbers. Someone'll be in touch for statements once this all settles."

Minutes later, two officers rushed past them, disappearing into the building. The Chief turned to the group, his tone more serious. "Any bodies we find in the halls, you're cleared of. But we need to see something upstairs."

Black's stomach tightened. He glanced at Professor Moore, who had gone pale. "What's going on?" she asked.

The Chief didn't answer. He led them to her floor, pausing outside her apartment. The door was slightly ajar, swinging on its hinges. Moore's eyes widened in panic. "What is this?" she whispered, fear creeping into her voice.

The Chief nudged the door open with his boot, revealing the chest from the basement, sitting in the middle of the living room like an unwelcome guest. He crossed the room and lifted the lid. Inside, the body lay exactly as they had left it—knife still protruding from its chest.

He picked up a photograph from the table, glancing at Moore. "Is this your apartment, ma'am?"

Moore shook her head frantically. "No, no, wait—"

"You're cleared of any bodies in the halls," the Chief said, his voice cool. "But this is a different story. This looks like evidence of a crime."

Before she could protest, the Chief nodded to his officers. They moved in, cuffing her without a word. Moore's eyes darted to Black, her face a mask of betrayal.

"Now you've lost everything," Black said quietly, his gaze cold.

He and the others stepped out of the apartment, leaving her to be taken away, her cries fading into the background as they exited the building. Outside, Black turned to Chioma, offering a nod. "Thanks for the help. Stay in touch."

Chioma smirked, gripping his cricket bat. "Anytime."

Black then faced Yehohanan, his expression softer. "Thanks for sticking around. If you need anything—job, place to stay—let me know."

Yehohanan nodded, his voice low. "I'll take you up on that."

And with that, the night closed in around them.

The End

EXCERPT OF MURDER IN
FROGTOWN

"So, this is one for the books." Black mumbled to himself scrolling through text messages as he waited for the train to rock to a stop at the Union Depot station in St. Paul, MN.

He had become a cliché, something he promised himself that he wouldn't do when he entered the P.I. trade years ago. He was trailing a man from Chicago, a suspected cheater, hired by the man's girlfriend. The entire situation put him in mind of the old retro private dick shows from back in the day, shows like Mannix, Kojak, or Mike Hammer Private Eye.

It was ludicrous to him that cases of this nature still existed, with social media and GPS tracking in phones it was easier than ever for spouses to catch their disloyal significant others in their *sneaky link hook-ups* nowadays. Black had charged the young ebony woman almost triple the rate he normally charged hoping she would turn it down, being that he didn't want to take the case even though he needed the money.

Things weren't looking so good after his run-in with the Ghost-face Killaz, a mid-level street gang in Chicago, they had proven more resourceful than Black had anticipated, a scandal and his reputation soiled, business wasn't as prosperous as it had once been, but he couldn't come across as desperate. When she didn't bat an eye at the price he tacked on expenses as well.

The train jolted to a stop, Black watched from a few seats away as the man he was following Kent Keach stood and exited the train. The man wasn't very observant, it was a wonder he hadn't noticed Black following him from his office in downtown Chicago to another state. Black stood and exited as well, the man he was following was a bit older than the woman he was supposedly cheating on, older by at least twenty years.

The client was a twenty-one-year-old bronze-colored black female. The cheater was a gray-haired, fake n bake tanned, Brooks Brothers suit-wearing middle-aged real estate investor from the wealthy side of the tracks. He was careful not to leave too much of a digital trail, instead of ordering an Uber he hopped in one of the yellow taxis sitting out front, Black followed suit and hopped in the taxi behind his, handed the driver a hundred-dollar bill. "Follow that cab." Black shook his head, one cliché after another.

The trip took only eight minutes, and they were pulling up in front of a duplex on Van Buren Ave. "Pull a few houses ahead of the taxi and park." Black demanded as he held up his phone with the camera on held it slightly above his head so that he could catch a view of Keach behind them getting out of his cab, the driver put the car in park and let the engine idle.

"What part of town are we in?" Black asked, eyes still glued to his phone watching Keach as he stood in front of the home appearing to be waiting for someone. "Not quite downtown, not quite the East

Side, they call it Frogtown." The driver answered in a strong middle eastern accent.

He kept the meter running. Black stopped looking at his phone long enough to take an assessment of the neighborhood. It wasn't Manhattan, but it wasn't O Block in Chicago either.

"What kind of people live around here?" Black asked taking note of young black mothers walking past pushing babies in strollers on one side of the street but up the block young white millennials jogging and walking Norfolk Terriers and Corgis. New homes were nestled or being built in between ran down homes or abandoned properties.

"When I first moved here twenty years ago it was mostly black people, always a mixture of white, black, Asian, Somali, but always mostly black, the neighborhood is getting better now."

Black was working on picking his battles, the old him would have corrected him or checked him about the racists' statement. But that wasn't why he was there, he learned that it wasn't his job to school the ignorant or willingly stupid. "What is it now?" Black asked, already knowing the answer.

"Blacks are moving out to Arden Hills, Little Canada, and Roseville, all suburbs won't be long before those areas are bad too but over here new homes are being developed, coffee shops, and such real nice it is still a mixture of all but mostly white people."

Maybe the client was right, Black thought to himself as a woman stepped out of the home, also pretty, also black, and just as young as the client she hugged Keach, and they began walking away hand in hand. "He has a type." Black said more to himself than to the driver.

"What?"

Black opened the door and got out, closing the door behind him he followed the couple matching their stroll. They were a few blocks ahead of Black at the corner when a jogger passed Black coming from behind him almost at an angle, he was average height and weight, brown skinned man, he wore an Itachi Uchiha face mask, the character from an anime show, the past year had been crazy a worldwide pandemic had occurred, one more excuse to divide the United States. Black vs. White, rich vs. poor, working-class vs. elitists, right vs. left, man vs. woman, and now those who wanted the quarantining and the dying and everything covid to stop vs. the anti-vaxxers. It was ending; a vaccine was being distributed but some still chose to wear masks when out in public.

Black-eyed the couple as the man reached them, instead of going around he stopped at an arm's length of the couple, removed a .38 revolver from his windbreaker aimed at the back of Keach's head, and pulled the trigger. The gunshot rang out, the woman screamed as his blood hit her face and she was pulled down with him when his frame slumped. She covered her head and cowered in fear, as the shooter, took aim at her.

"Aye!" Black yelled out as he ran towards the shooter. The shooter paused, looked back towards where Black was running from, tucked the gun back into his jacket, and ran away. By the time Black made it to the woman and Keach when he looked in the direction the man had run off in, he was nowhere in sight.

***

The woman and Black stood down the block in front of the woman's home waiting for the police to arrive. Her hand shook as she held a cigarette to her lips, eyes glued to the corpse. Black had a lot of questions he wanted to ask; his cheating spouse case had possibly just turned into a homicide. He needed to get answers before the police arrived, he knew he was running out of time but didn't want to press her either.

He let a few beats pass before confronting her. "You mind telling me your name ma'am?" She took another pull from her cigarette, blew out the smoke. Black cleared his throat. Spoke again. "My name is Black, like the color."

She turned her attention to Black, rolled her eyes took another pull from her cigarette before dropping it on the ground and stomping out the flame. "I know what colors are."

Black smirked. "Of course, and your name is?"

"Why?"

"I just want to help." She looked Black up and down, pulled another cigarette from her pack, and lit it.

"I know this can be traumatizing but-"

"But what, you the police or something just let me think you keep asking me all these got damn questions, damn let me gather my bearings."

Black nodded that he understood. After finishing her second cigarette, the police had finally arrived on the scene. Neighbors stood in front of their homes or on their porches watching no one brave enough to approach the body littering the corner of their block. Police approached from both ends of the block, you would think that it was a full-on riot, eight squad cars swarmed the block officers hopping out, they moved aggressively towards Black and the woman whom he still had yet to learn her name.

"Are either of you the one that made the 9-11 call?" The officer asked, hand on his gun. Black shook his head no. "No."

"You want to tell us what happened?"

Before Black could respond the woman, who was once too reserved to talk interrupted.

"Cydney, Cydney Doyle, OMG I was standing right next to him when it happened...I." The floodgates opened and her face was covered in tears, Black watched as the officer attempted to console her.

A female officer approached and took Black to the side to question him. "May I ask you, your name sir?"

"Black, Black Love." The officer raised her head from taking notes in her notepad, eyed Black. "No time for games, not your street name, the name your mama gave you."

Black folded his arms across his chest. "That is the name my mama gave me, Black is my first name, Love is my last name."

She went back to jotting in her notepad. "How did you know the deceased?"

"I didn't."

"What about the woman, you two together?"

"Nope."

"You got an ID on you?" Black reached into his pocket and removed his wallet handing her his driver's license and his P.I. card. She looked at both, looked at him then tucked both into the back flap of her notepad. "Illinois huh, you working a case?"

"I am."

"That guy laying on the ground it?"

"He is."

"Stay, here I'll be right back."

Black nodded that he understood as she turned and went to one of the squad cars, he assumed to run his name for warrants. He watched the interaction of the police with Cydney Doyle, and every now and then he looked over at the officer with his identification. After several minutes she returned and handed him his ID.

"You have no warrants and your P.I.'s license is valid. I just got off the phone with the sergeant on duty how come you didn't alert someone at the department about what you were out here doing?"

"I don't have any legal obligation to report to any law enforcement agency local or federal."

"True, but next time you may want to do it as a professional courtesy."

Black tucked his ID back into his wallet.

"How much longer will this take?"

"Not much longer, a homicide detective should be here soon, you mind telling us about the case you're working on?"

"I do."

"Did you get a good look at the shooter?"

Black shook his head no. "Nah, I was trailing the couple, this guy wearing a black tracksuit anime face mask comes from behind me jogging, passes me up, he didn't seem to be in a rush he jogged at a comfortable pace, I paid him no mind. He gets close to the couple, boom, one to the back of the head, Keach goes down, the woman goes down the shooter points the gun at her she screams, I yell at him and sprint in that direction he sees me coming gets spooked and sprints off before he does the girl all I saw was the back of his head."

"You armed Love?"

"No."

"You ran after an active shooter unarmed?"

Black smirked. "Yeah, fight or flight, right?"

The officer closed the notepad. "Wait here, the detective will be here shortly."

Black nodded. The officer walked off.

***

Black leaned against a chain-link fence talking on the phone with Trigger as he waited for the detectives to arrive. Stone was his on-again-off-again *friend* with benefits now they were more friendly and fewer benefits they had been playing this game of back and forth for a few years now and had taken a hiatus on the physical part of their relationship.

"I say just come home; case closed that situation has nothing to do with you."

"Yeah, but."

"You don't like leaving things unresolved."

Black cracked a smile. "I don't like leaving things unresolved."

"Don't make this like Lagos all over again."

"Trust me."

"Just be safe Black."

"No doubt."

He ended the call as two-average height, blonde-haired, guys wearing almost identical colored blue suits approached. Both men's facial expressions were almost robotic-like. "Mr. Love, I am detective Beckett, this is Washington, we'd like to ask you a few questions."

Black nodded in agreement as he watched Cydney Doyle being placed in the back of a squad car. She wasn't in handcuffs, but she was being escorted away. Black turned his attention back to the detective speaking. "How long have you been in town?"

"Maybe almost two hours."

"What brought you to St. Paul?"

"As I told the patrol officer, I'm registered as a P.I. in the state of Illinois I was trailing Mr. Keach for a client."

"That client's name?"

"Is this necessary?"

"Just want to clear some things up that's all, we have two people here from Illinois one ends up dead just have to be sure you're here doing what you said you were here to do."

"I didn't have to stick around; I could have left before you got here."

"And we thank you for not fleeing the scene of a crime, and if you could show more cooperation and answer our questions, we'll get this settled and you can be on your way."

A call came through on the radio of the other detective who had yet to speak. He stepped a few feet away to respond to the call. A few seconds later he returned to where Black and the other detective were. He removes his firearm and aims it at Black.

"I'm going to need you to place your hands behind your head."

"What the fuck is this?" Black asked hands still at his side.

"I will not ask again sir, place your hands behind your head."

Black raised his hands, and the other officer handcuffed him. "You are being placed under arrest for the murder of Kent Keach."

"What, you have to be kidding me."

"Ms. Doyle told us what happened, she told the patrol officer you and Mr. Keach got into a heated argument, they walked away, and you shot him in the back of the head."

Black laughed. "What kind of backwater, redneck, made for TV drama kind of police work is this? I did not kill her lover."

They placed him in the back of the car. "Cut the crap, you know that wasn't her lover, it was her father."

***

Black had been sitting in the interrogation room for almost four hours, he had yet to give the detectives any real substantial answers to the questions he was being asked. It was a stall tactic to keep from being officially booked and transported to lock up. He knew if he told them anything of any substance, he may unintentionally incriminate himself guilty or not. He also knew that if he invoked his right to remain silent there would be no reason to keep him there and he would be immediately transferred to lock up.

He was killing time, waiting for his attorney to arrive. When it looked as if they were beginning to lose patience with him the door opened, and his attorney walked in followed by the chief of police, the district attorney, and the attorney general of Minnesota.

"Detectives, I am Attorney General Malone of Illinois, I am acting as counsel for Mr. Love. Your chief has briefed me with the particulars of this case, and it is of my understanding that there was no weapon found on the suspect or in the surrounding areas?"

"No ma'am but we have an eyewitness that says-."

"Did you run a test for gunpowder residue on my client's hands and or clothing? It is of my understanding that Mr. Love told the responding officer that interviewed him that he was at least two blocks away when the shooting occurred, if he was the one to commit said crime then surely gun powder residue would be on his clothing and hands."

"Uh, no ma'am we have not."

"Detectives, uncuff my client, Mr., Love will relinquish his clothing, and allow the St. Paul police forensic team to run a test for gunpowder residue on his hands and I request that he be released immediately."

The two detectives looked at one another flabbergasted.

"You heard the attorney general gentlemen get those cuffs off of him, one of you get him an SPD sweatsuit to change into and an evidence bag for his things I will personally escort him and AG Malone to forensics." The attorney general for Minnesota said as he turned and exited the room.

***

"No more favors Black." Veronica said as she climbed into the back of the Towne car closed the door and pulled off.

Black stood on the corner watching as the car drove away. He looked down at the clothes he was wearing. "I need to get to a store and get out of these police clothes." He said to himself as he logged into his phone and called an Uber. He pulled up the nearest clothing store on Google. After making it to the store just before they closed, he changed and caught another Uber back to Cydney Doyle's place.

He knew he should have listened to Trigger and now to Veronica's advice and headed back to Chicago he knew he would not live with himself if he didn't get to the bottom of this, he had to find out why she lied. On the drive over he called his client, the line was disconnected. Something fishy was going on. Thirty minutes later he was climbing out of the vehicle in front of Cydney's on Van Buren.

He looked down the street at where the murder had taken place only a bloodstain remained. He opened the gate and walked into the yard. Being that it was a duplex he wasn't sure which she had come out of, he tried the place on the right first. Ringing the bell, then knocking on the door when there was no answer, he peeked through the window to find a body lying on the floor. He twists the doorknob to find it unlocked, crept in, and made his way to the body on the floor.

It was Cydney, he checked her pulse when she was unresponsive, he reached for his phone to dial the police. The floor creaked behind him he whipped his head around just as someone was coming at him with a knife, Black blocked the attack flipping the man over his shoulder, Black whipped around and faced the man lying on his back staring up at him he was wearing the same Itachi Uchiha face mask as the shooter, it couldn't be a coincidence.

The attacker made it back to his feet rushed Black, they locked arms, he was bigger than Black in height and weight, but he was no fighter. Black was. Arms still locked, Black pulled the man towards him simultaneously throwing jabs to his ribs with his knee, in the middle of the scuffle his mask came off and fell to the floor. Four quick blows and the man let loose, dropping to his knees, Black took a step back.

"Stay down." Before Black could react, he pulled a gun and fired a shot above Black's head.

"Don't look at me!" He yelled out as he got to his feet and ran past Black bumping into him knocking him from his feet, out the front door leaving his mask.

Black picked up the mask the black cloth was covered in face make-up. He stuffed it into his pocket and rushed to the front door, standing on the porch he watched as a car turned the corner. He was too late; he had more questions than answers he didn't want a round two with the police so he went back inside and wiped down anything he may have touched and gone out the back door.

***

Walking the streets in a town that he was unfamiliar with he found himself sitting at a table in a bar called Willards. Looked like a neighborhood watering hole, just like the cabbie described the Frogtown area a mixture of all: a group of women playing darts all Black, a mixed couple Black guy-Asian girl, all the pool tables filled with players two Black guys on one, and a Black guy and a white guy on the other. None of the people stood out, they all looked like blue collar workers unwinding after punching the clock at whatever they all did for a living.

Black ordered a beer and a burger and fries. He guzzled the beer before he finished his meal, ordered two more. He people watched, some of the people wore face masks, most didn't. He removed the mask from his pocket and placed it on the table in front of him. The waitress was a five-foot even Tia and Tamara look-a-like she wore her hair in box braids, cut-off jean shorts with holes in the front, short sleeve white button-up tied in a knot at the bottom. She was something nice to ogle over as he let the thoughts of the day run through his mind.

She checked in on him from time to time to see if he needed anything else to drink. They made small talk, in between her tending to other customers. Black took note of her green eyes, they stuck out in the dimly lit room. Now on his fourth beer, he found himself letting his eyes wander from her eyes to her lips, down to her neck and her breasts, down to her thighs that the cut-offs clung to perfectly. She smiled.

"Uh, my eyes are up here."

Black smiled back. "I know, I ain't looking at your eyes right now, I'm trying to see something else."

"Is that right?" Black took another sip from his beer. Looked up at her face. "You have something on your collar."

She sat the tray she was carrying down on his table, pulled her collar so that it was eye level. "I hate wearing white."

"Why, it looks good on you."

"Damn, make-up."

Black shrugged his shoulders. "I'm sure that happens, working hard, busy, moving fast it gets on your shirt."

"It's not from my face, it's from my neck."

"You put make-up on your neck?"

She placed both of her hands' palms up in front of Black so that he could see them. On both wrists, there was a splotch of missing pigmentation. "I have vitiligo, it's still new to me, only been a year since the symptoms started showing up. In my mind I know it's nothing to be ashamed of but the vain part of me covers my neck with makeup to match my natural skin tone."

Black smiled. "Well, you must not be that vain, you told me a stranger you could have just rolled with the make-up from the face story I put out there and left it at that."

"Yeah, well, I'm a work in progress can I get you another beer?"

Black stared down at the mask, pulled fifty dollars from his pocket sat it on the table picked up the mask, and rushed from the bar.

***

Back out on the streets, Black found himself back at the scene of the crime once again. He had expected to find the streets flooded with police once again, but no one had called. He started at the end of the block where Keach had been killed and made his way down the block towards Cydney's looking at each home's front door, once passing Cydney's and making it to the end of the block he crossed the street and did the same again looking at each door at all the homes. Satisfied that he had found what he was looking for he called an Uber.

***

Riding in the back of the Uber he furiously clicked away on his cell sending messages to Seshat, his hacker. He had helped her out of a legal situation years ago, she had been helping him out with cases ever since. He had a hunch at how to identify the shooter, but nothing else was making sense and the messages that Seshat was sending him back were filling in the empty spaces. By the time he was pulling up to the police station, he had it all but solved, in theory, anyway. He got out of the car went into the station and asked for detectives Beckett and Washington. After waiting more than thirty minutes he was shown to an interrogation room and shortly after the detectives showed up.

"What can we do for you, Mr. Love?"

"I know who killed Keach and Doyle."

One of the detectives leaned down on the table. "Doyle, Doyle's dead?"

"Yeah, found her knifed to death at her place."

"What were you doing at her place?"

"Working my case."

"Your case ended when Keach got killed."

"I don't walk away from a case unfinished, not my style."

The other detective spoke up. "You said you know who did it, who?"

"Steven Duke."

"And who the hell is Steven Duke?"

"Keach's son-in-law."

"Wait a minute Doyle didn't say anything about being married."

"She wasn't, it was my client's husband Kaneisha Jones."

"Are you telling us that your client Kaneisha Jones was Keach's daughter as well?"

"Yeah, he liked to get around."

"What was the motive? Why the games, though she said it was her lover?"

Black slid his phone across the table to the detective. "I had my people do some digging, Keach was worth eight figures, he had a wife and kids and Kaneisha and Cydney were outside kids."

The detective picked up the phone and began scrolling through the message that Black had received from Seshat. "What am I looking at?"

"Those are PDFs of results from an ancestry DNA test linking my client to Keach."

He sat the phone down on the table. "Wait, none of this is connecting."

"Keach was dying, pick up the phone go to the next message, those are copies of his medical reports. He was amending his will to add Kaneisha with his other kids from his marriage."

He picked up the phone and looked at the message. "I'm not going to even ask you how you got his medical records, but this makes no sense why kill him if she was already being added?"

"Had my colleagues with the Chicago PD stop by her place to pick her up before I got here, they searched her place and found a list of names of other people we're theorizing that they were all Keach's children."

The detective laughed. "A hit list?" Black shrugged. He continued. "This Kaneisha, had her husband follow you to Chicago kill Keach and Cydney before the will was amended?"

"He's no killer, I'm thinking he screwed up and hit Doyle by accident."

"How do you place him at the scene?"

"The phone." The detective picks it up again and goes to the next message. "While I was at Cydney's me and Duke tussled a bit, his mask came off." Black pulled the mask from his pocket and placed it on the table.

"You removed evidence from a homicide scene?"

"I know I screwed up but, look at the mask."

The other detective picked up the mask and looked at it. "What is it, make-up?"

"Exactly, show your partner my phone." He showed his partner the phone. "It's a Facebook page of Duke from what a year ago and?"

"Look closely at his neck, he has the first signs of vitiligo."

"Yeah and?"

"Go to the next pic in my phone, no vitiligo, that's from last month. Vitiligo doesn't go away, that's make-up to match his natural skin tone. And before you ask, go to the next message it's footage from the homes across the street from Doyle's place captured from the neighbor's Ring cameras it's from an hour before we arrived at her place Duke walking past wearing the tracksuit and no mask. Go to the next message it's footage of him running past me the same tracksuit with the mask that's lying on the table."

"That still doesn't tell us why Doyle lied on you?"

Black held out his hand for his phone. The detective hesitated before handing it back. "I emailed everything I just showed you to your chief, being that I didn't obtain it in the most by the book way I'll let you do the leg work and get warrants for the footage from the neighbors, do what you will with the mask, it's also tainted evidence. As far as the motive for her lying on me." Black stood and walked toward the door. "That's for you to find out, I can't do all of your work for you." He nodded at both men, opened the door, and walked out.

***

ABOUT THE AUTHOR

Antwan Floyd Sr. is an American novelist, most widely recognized for his crime fiction. He has written a series of best-selling mysteries featuring the hard-boiled detective Black Love, a black private investigator living in Chicago, IL; they are perhaps his most popular works.